Published 2008

Morgan-Bradley Productions
Seattle, USA

ISBN-10: 0-9799377-0-1
ISBN-13: 978-0-9799377-0-5

Printed in the United States of America

First Edition June 2008
10 9 8 7 6 5 4 3 2 1
OPM

Foreword

I have taken several contemporary issues or topics of debate and woven them within the context of a 19th century mystery/adventure western.

The hero and heroine's view of the world in this story is where a person has the "right" to take individual action and that the letter of the law is somehow corrupted unless guided by the spirit of the law. Also, they are not plagued by indecisiveness and self-doubt.

So…curl up and enjoy!

For Gus (my faithful Shih-Tzu)
whose Spirit lives on!

The Adventures of Jim McClair
Spirit of the Law

Jim stepped down from the train onto the dusty board walk. It had been a long trip coming from Missouri to Montana, but a few more days on horseback and he would be able to rest while waiting to see John Wilson, the Territorial Governor. Wilson had telegraphed a few weeks ago and said he needed Jim's help with a problem in the western part of the territory.

Stepping aside to let other passengers off, Jim reflected on his past relationship with Wilson. They had ramrodded together over in the panhandle of Texas in their younger days, fought side by side during the last couple years in the war of northern aggression, and then parted company to each find their own calling.

Since then, Wilson had worked his way into politics and had his sights set on being elected Governor when Montana got around to becoming a state, while he had spent the years traveling through the Midwest and the eastern Rockies, mostly in the southern Colorado area.

As his thoughts drifted back to the war, Jim remembered the grim role he had played. His talent for long distance shooting had been noticed and he was ordered to be the company sniper. Professionally he had few equals, but personally he had considered the job to be an unpleasant and gruesome one.

Smiling to himself, Jim remembered a time he had felt an ironic satisfaction using his skills. He had been attached to the remnants of a battalion of Confederate soldiers fortified on one side of a river; with two Union Company's entrenched on the opposite bank. Every few days the Confederate Major or the Union Colonel would send a squad of soldiers across the river to harass the other side. Obviously, the survival rate was pretty much zero, and the senseless war of attrition was serving no purpose other than to kill young men under both commands and demoralize the troops.

One time while talking to Wilson, who was a Captain and aide to the Major, Jim had asked why both sides didn't just withdraw. The war was almost over, so why not have a local cease fire and wait until hostilities had formally ended. Then the remaining troops could head back to whatever might be left of their homes and families.

Wilson explained the Major had grand delusions about dying to the last man for the southern cause and wouldn't even discuss a truce. And their commander, Colonel Hightower, was apparently just as loony as the Major. Wilson had met Hightower before the war, and said the man approached every situation like he was on a personal mission from God.

"Take my word for it, Jim. We're caught between a rock and a hard place. If we walk out on the Major, the Union boys will hunt us down one at a time, and if we mutiny, we'll still have to deal with the enemy."

Thinking about it while they smoked and drank coffee one evening, Jim had an idea. "I think I might have found a solution to this insanity, John. You're his aide, suppose you appeal to the arrogance of our Major and get him to meet their Colonel. Convince the Major to go out and ask Hightower to surrender, or retreat. And when Hightower hears the offer to meet, he will think the Major is planning to offer terms of surrender."

Wilson looked up with a puzzled expression on his face. "You know that won't do any good, Jim. So what do you really have in mind?"

"You're going to have to trust me on this one, John. Just see if you can do it."

A couple days later, a runner under a white flag delivered an offer to meet the Union commander in the middle of the only remaining bridge. This one had not been destroyed because each side had thoughts of using it after they won.

On the morning of the scheduled meeting, Jim slipped out of camp with two rifles and positioned himself on a wooded hill about 300 yards from the bridge.

Noticing activity along the banks of the river, Jim raised his field glasses to watch. As the two officers approached the bridge, he could almost see the self-righteous contempt in their eyes. When the commanders and their aides started walking out to meet each other, he checked both loads in the rifles, and waited until they stopped a few feet from each other.

Knowing the Confederate side was weaker, and would delay any reaction for awhile, he sighted in on the Major. His plan had to be flawless or it would be a total disaster. So while he was used to taking clean headshots, he figured to play it safe and aim for the center of their bodies.

Since he was on an angle behind the Major, there was no way to hit him from the front. Situations like this had always puzzled Jim about the rules of conduct in war. Gallantry demanded that you face your opponent head on, but as a sniper he was expected to take out enemies regardless of what they were doing or where they were.

There was no difference, from a sniper's point of view, whether a soldier was taking a leak by the side of the road or engaged in actual combat. He had never understood if the seemingly endless list of contradictions were the normal result of a huge bureaucracy or simply the introduction of twisted outlooks by people as they gained power and influence.

Realizing this wasn't the time to be philosophical; Jim aimed between the Major's shoulder blades and squeezed off a round. Quickly dropping that rifle, he picked up the other one. Swinging the loaded one into position, he was aware the Major was down and the Union Colonel had frozen for a second in surprise. It flashed through his mind the Colonel probably thought one of his own men had done it.

Before the Colonel could react, Jim sighted in on the medals on his chest and fired. This time he watched to see what would happen. No rifle fire came from either bank...the troops were probably stunned at what they had just witnessed.

The two aides had gone out unarmed, so they just looked at each other in shock. Eventually, Jim could make out they were gesturing with their hands and saying something to one another. At last they stepped forward, shook hands, and walked back to their respective side of the river. He had no clue what had transpired between the two men, but something had, because neither side started firing after the aides got back to their lines.

Later, Wilson found Jim by a campfire smoking a cigarette and sat down across from him. Rolling his own smoke, Wilson finally paused and looked over at him and started laughing.

"What the hell's so funny?" Jim asked.

"Well, it was the strangest thing you ever saw. Of

course you were probably just sleeping in late and didn't see what happened, right Jim? Anyway, there we were standing on the bridge, and the Major had just started to ask the Colonel to surrender, when he got killed. Before anybody could do anything, the Colonel went down also."

"There I was standing by my dead Major while the other aide was standing by his dead Colonel. After recovering from the initial shock, I told him we weren't interested in continuing this bullshit and they could have the damn bridge. Also, what was left of our unit would be traveling in the opposite direction.

The Colonel's aide looked at me for a few seconds and then smiled. He said their men didn't care about the bridge either, or the stupid fight, and would be heading back to join the main Union Army. Then he wished me luck and we shook hands and parted company."

"Things seem to be looking up for the men," Jim commented wryly.

Later, after assuming formal command of the unit, Wilson told the troops of his plan and everyone prepared to move out. The mood in camp was light and it felt like a heavy burden had been removed from the men's shoulders.

A few miles down the road, after the scouts reported the Union soldiers were marching in the other direction, Wilson halted and assembled the troops. Then he informed the men that his last order was for them to get rid of their uniforms and go their own way. "The war is over for us, boys."

A piercing blast from the train's whistle broke Jim's thoughts and he shook his head to clear the memories. Looking around at the sleepy little community, there didn't seem to be any place to sleep here before heading out on horseback. The town had about a dozen homes, a general store, and the standard saloon. Also, somewhere in the distance, he could hear the hammer of a black-smith ringing off the steel anvil.

As he walked back to the boxcar that held his horse, Whisper, he noticed a couple of young ladies stepping down from the passenger car to stretch their legs. He tipped his hat to them, said "good morning" and started walking past. One of the ladies called out and asked if he was going farther on the train.

Pausing, Jim studied her, "No ma'am, I'm going to continue the rest of the journey by horse."

She hesitated and smiled, "Then I guess I had better introduce myself before you leave. My name is Marge, and this is my traveling companion and friend, Callie."

"It's a pleasure meeting the two of you. I'm Jim Mc-Clair and I can truly say I'm sorry to have to forego the pleasure of getting further acquainted with you and your friend."

"Listen to his fancy talk boys."

Jim turned and faced three men lounging by the load-ing platform. He was always puzzled when strangers confronted him. After all, he was over six feet tall and tipped the scales at 220 pounds. He guessed it was the tied down colt 45.s that gave misfits like these courage.

None of them looked like cowpunchers in town for the day to visit the saloon, so he was a little curious what they were doing at the train station. Maybe they were waiting for someone or just bored and looking for troub-le. Whatever the reason, he didn't like to be bothered. Where did these morons keep coming from anyway, he wondered? Jim gave the men a cold look, "I take it you men are too ignorant to understand polite conversation."

The man in the middle stepped forward, "Are you talking to me?"

"Well, since you answered, then at least you have enough brains to know how stupid you are."

The man lowered his hand to the butt of his gun, "Nobody says something like that to Steve Wilcox and lives. Nobody!"

"Listen mister," Jim snapped. "I don't care about your name, what you think or what your problems are. Furthermore, I certainly don't want to look at you, let alone listen to you. So draw, or take your friends over to the saloon and get out of my sight."

Steve demonstrated his intentions by attempting to draw. He had barely cleared leather when a slug from Jims' colt smashed a hole through his forehead, blowing blood and brains all over the loading dock. Jim holstered his gun and asked, "Do you two want to bother me also, or go have a quiet drink and be thankful you're alive?"

The older, slim man on the right quickly spoke up. "No mister, things got a little out of hand and we'll be going right now."

Just then a man wearing a badge came up. "What the hell is going on here? I'm Sheriff Hill and I was in town checking on things when I heard a gunshot."

The younger, heavy set man blurted out, "We were just making fun of his fancy talk when he pulled his gun on Steve and shot him, sheriff."

"What's your name, Mister?" the sheriff asked.

"Jim McClair."

"Well McClair, in this county I keep a tight rein on problem people, so just hand over your gun. Then you'll be riding back with me to the county courthouse, over in

Meadow Springs, until we clear up this shooting."

"I don't think so," Jim replied, with an intent, calm look in his eyes. "You know these men aren't cow-punchers and you show up after the fact and think you're going to railroad a stranger just getting into this one horse town? What I suggest sheriff, is you ask some of these other people what happened before you go off half-cocked."

The sheriff looked nervously at Jim, noticing he did not seem upset or afraid. Maybe trying to buffalo this stranger wasn't going to go down so well. The sheriff considered what Jim said and asked loudly, "Did anyone else see or hear what happened?"

Marge stepped forward and spoke up, "I was here sheriff and here's what happened. Jim McClair and I were just beginning to have a friendly conversation when these men made fun of him. They had words and Jim told Steve to draw or leave. Steve grabbed for his gun, and…I guess you can see who lost."

Callie stepped forward and added, "That's the way it happened sheriff."

The sheriff paused and contemplated his bad luck in picking today to swing through this sorry excuse for a town. "You'll still have to come to the courthouse and give me a written statement."

Jim shook his head patiently, "Sheriff, with all due respect, you can go write up what the ladies and I told you. If you still have questions, you can wire me in care of John Wilson. You do know how to contact him, don't you?"

The sheriff got a sick feeling in his guts. "You do mean John Wilson, the Territorial Governor?"

"That's the one."

The sheriff thought for a moment. "You're free to go, but it would be real nice if you didn't stay around, not only for your health, but for my peace of mind."

"Thanks sheriff, I'll be out of your county by this evening." Turning back to the ladies, he asked where they were headed.

"Callie and I are going to Helena, how about you?" Marge asked.

"That's where I'm heading also. Maybe I'll see you there in a few days."

Callie looked at him quizzically, "Why spend days on your horse when you can be there on the train by tomorrow?"

"Because I want to get a feel for this part of the country again and I can't do that from a train. Also, I've been cooped up with too many people for longer than I like and I need a break."

Marge smiled coyly and said seductively, "I'll be watching for your arrival, Jim."

Not sure how to respond to the sultry tone in her voice, he bid the ladies farewell and went to get Whisper from the box car. After saddling his horse, he tied down a long slender wood case behind the saddle. As Whisper stepped eagerly away from the train, he glanced back to see Marge and Callie waving to him. He tipped his hat and then turned his horse west. Several days of being on the train had made both man and horse restless, so he decided to let Whisper have some fun and gallop a couple of miles before slowing him down to a walk.

The miles drifted past, and Jim was glad he had gotten off the train. Listening to strangers talking loudly around him, as if anyone else cared what they had to say, and frustrated children bawling, was enough to drive a

13

person crazy.

He preferred this wide open country. There weren't a lot of trees around, except down by the creeks and rivers, but it was still beautiful in its' own way. The sun was just beginning to lower over the far mountains and the shadow effect gave them a purplish hazy look. The thin, distant clouds were a brilliant red with shades of pink along the edges, and made Jim think of the crowns that royalty wore. Certainly, whoever had written about "purple mountain majesties" could only have done so if they had seen something like this firsthand.

Seeing a large stand of cottonwoods down by a small creek, he decided this would be a good place to camp for the night. Ground hitching his horse, he collected some rocks to place around a small campfire. After getting a fire going, he put the coffee pot and skillet on the stones and waited for everything to heat up. When the skillet seemed hot enough he threw in several slices of bacon. Just before it was finished he placed some cold biscuits on top to warm up, and then poured himself a cup of strong coffee.

It was kind of strange. When he was in town at a café or hotel he liked milk and sugar in his coffee. But out here in the solitude of nature he enjoyed the straight black flavor of it. Later, after eating several biscuit and bacon sandwiches, he poured himself another cup and rolled a smoke while he watched the fire die down.

When there were only a few embers left, he walked over and checked on Whisper and brought his bedroll back. He knew his horse would alert him if anything or anyone approached. So after laying out his bedding, he stretched out and laid there enjoying the peaceful nightfall.

14

Looking up at the millions of twinkling stars he soon located the big and little dipper, but that was about all he knew of the constellations in the sky. The quiet solitude, broken only by the sound of crickets and an occasional frog, helped him relax and his thoughts went back to Marge.

She was some looker…that was for sure. And her smile had made him feel like a clumsy teenager. Thinking pleasant thoughts of what it might be like to hold her in his arms, he drifted off into a contented sleep.

With the dawns early light, Jim was already up and getting ready to move out. He let Whisper drink his fill of water while he smoked a cigarette, and then started riding in a northwesterly direction.

Jim was in no real hurry to get to Helena. Wilson would be waiting, but from the telegram the problem sounded like it had been around for a while and could certainly wait a few more days. Besides, he needed more than a couple of nights to relax and unwind.

Lately, he often found his thoughts drifting to the idea of a place to settle down, hopefully with a good woman. Smiling, he thought of Marge…there was a piece of cake! Maybe he'd see her again in Helena.

Reflecting on the time since he had last seen Wilson, made Jim think about all the years he had spent traveling. Years of hard work before joining the confederate army and the many years of hard living since had kept him in good shape, and he knew he could still hold his own against the cocky young bucks out to prove their manhood.

To be honest, the years since the war had not been that hard. Shortly after he and Wilson had parted company, Jim had been riding through a desolate area between Louisiana and Texas when he came upon some burned out wagons.

From the looks of things it must have been a confederate convoy heading towards Texas. The dead soldiers had been scavenged by wild animals, and there was no longer the stench of death around, so the wagons must have been ambushed quite a while ago.

Knowing he had not seen any sign of people for quite

some time, he felt safe and tied his horse to a small tree and wandered over to the wagons to have a look around. It couldn't have been Indians who had attacked, because the secret compartments for holding gold or other valuables had been ripped open and were empty. That left either outlaws or Union soldiers.

But whoever had done this was not aware the South had so many convoys ambushed that there were a lot of wagons built with two secret compartments. The first one was expected to be found, and a reasonable amount of gold or silver would be placed in it. If the convoy was ambushed and overwhelmed, then the attackers would find this loot and ride off thinking they had cleaned out the wagons.

The South had started using, towards the end of the war, secondary compartments in a variety of places. One tricky location was inside hollowed out spare axles. This is where the bulk of the gold or silver would be stashed for safekeeping or recovery. The only reason Jim knew about this method of transport was because he had been friends with Wilson who had been privy to a lot of secrets about government operations.

Moving among the wagons he saw all of the obvious hiding places had been opened up. Well, that only left the axles to check out. There were nine wagons and each held two spares. He took the top one off and laid it on the ground. Finding a rusted, but usable axe laying in the grass, he proceeded to chop it in half.

This one was solid wood, and he thought about whether he really wanted to keep chopping through axles in the hope of finding gold.

Pausing for a smoke, he considered the situation. Wagons actually did break axles, so there was always a potential need to replace them while traveling. However, each wagon had two spare wheels and axles, and as Jim thought about it, he realized there was no need to have double replacements, especially with axles. Also, if you did break one, it would be normal to walk over and take the top one first.

Getting excited, he went back and pulled the bottom axle out on the ground and proceeded to split it apart. Listening to the sound of the axe hitting the wood, he knew it was not solid all the way through. Finally, he chopped far enough into the wood to hear the axe blade striking metal.

Rolling the axle over, he finished chopping it in half and several twenty dollar gold eagles fell out. Lifting up the other end, a stream of coins poured out. He couldn't believe his good luck and started placing them in a sack. He knew there was no Confederate government to return the money to, and he damn sure wasn't handing it over to the Union.

Having made up his mind to keep the gold, it had taken him nearly three months to remove the rest of it and move it to a more accessible location. Then he had spent almost two years gradually getting the gold deposited in various banks and consolidated into three separate accounts.

While he hated progress, he knew as long as people were going to continue breeding like rabbits there would always be a steady stream of people heading west, if for no other reason than this was where the last great tracts of open land were still available.

Knowing transportation and communication was the key to moving men and materials; he invested almost half of the money into the Northern Pacific Railroad and

18

a Telegraph & Telephone Company. He had never seen a telephone, but figured anything that could let a person talk to someone else over long distances would probably catch on.

As a consequence of these investments, he earned over three thousand dollars a year in dividends. Considering the average cowboy made about three to four hundred a year, he felt pretty good about his financial situation. The rest he simply kept in reserve for the unexpected and for helping out the occasional person who deserved a break.

Looking around, Jim realized half the day had gone by while he reminisced, so he rode Whisper down to the creek and made a small fire for a coffee and cigarette break. While his horse cropped grass along the bank, he studied the land around him and tried to place where he was relative to Helena. He was north of the Yellowstone River, and figured he had already passed by Livingston, so he must still be two or three days ride from Helena.

After his horse drank some more water, and he had rinsed and filled the canteens, he started in a more northerly direction. The day passed uneventfully and Jim was feeling relaxed and thinking about what he would do when he reached Helena in a couple of days.

The first thing he planned on doing was getting a nice hotel room and having a hot bath! Then he would enjoy a big steak dinner and get a good nights sleep before letting Wilson know he was in town.

Not long after getting on the trail the next morning, he could hear the distant sound of occasional rifle fire and from the sound Jim knew it was Winchesters. Coming up over a low hill he came upon two men trotting their horses around, yelling and firing at small objects frantically running through the grass and shrubs.

Wondering what the men were shooting at, probably just prairie dogs, he studied the situation. Suddenly, he heard a yelp and heard one of the men shout that he had hit another one. Jim knew the sound of the animal in pain was a dog, and moved quickly forward.

Killing dogs that had gone wild was understandable, but those small furry objects had to be puppies, and this made his blood boil. Yelling to the men and waving his hat to get their attention, he rode up and asked what the hell was going on.

"It ain't none of your damn business, mister, but were having a little sport with these dogs," the wiry man on Jims' right said.

"They look like puppies to me," Jim replied, as he looked around in disgust. He could see two dead puppies, one dying, and another frightened one cowering under a small shrub. Pointing, he asked, "What's with the large dog lying over there?"

The man on the left swung his horse around to face Jim. "Now that was downright funny to watch. The big dog is the father and you should have seen him trying to protect his pups. We finally shot him, but he's still alive. We figured on letting him watch while we finished off the rest of his pups and then kill him too. But like Slim said, mister, it ain't none of your affair."

Jim silently counted to himself to bring his anger down. "What kind of pathetic men are you? Going around shooting dogs and puppies and thinking it's funny!"

From the sharp tone in his voice the men sidestepped their horses to spread apart. Slim spoke up, "You got no right coming up to a couple of strangers and telling them their business, mister."

Jim had seen Slim fire last, without reloading, so he concentrated on the one to his left. "When a man sees something wrong, it's his right and obligation to stand up and be counted," he replied.

As Slim started telling Jim what an asshole he was, the man on the left began to swing his Winchester across the saddle horn towards Jim.

Jim knew there was no such thing as a fast draw from horseback, but that smooth accurate firing was the important thing. Drawing his colt, he fired, killing the man instantly with a shot to the chest that must have exploded his heart.

Slim cursed and jumped his horse forward, as Jim swung his gun back and fired a hurried shot into his stomach. Pitching forward off the horse, Slim fell to the ground and began screaming.

Stepping down from Whisper, Jim walked over to the dying man and kicked his six-gun out of reach. Finally, Slims' screaming subsided to a low moan.

He looked up at Jim. "You're a real son of a bitch, doing this to me and my partner. Are you at least going to bury us, so the animals don't get to us?"

Surveying the scene around him, Jim asked if they had planned on burying the puppies after killing them.

"Hell no! Did you think we were going to bury them and say some words over their grave?" the man asked viciously.

"Well then, I think you have your answer, you can just rot out here in the wind and rain like you were planning on doing to those poor animals," Jim said calmly. Slim tried to spit at him, but only began vomiting up blood before falling back dead.

Working his way through the brush, Jim collected the dead puppies, and dug a common grave for all three of them. Not really knowing what to say about the senseless cruelty of some people, he left and walked over to the puppy hiding by the shrub.

He gently picked up the small dog and carried him over where his dad lay. The puppy wiggled free from his arms, and began whimpering and licking the face of the older dog. Kneeling down, Jim saw that the bullet had gone through the hip, and while the dog had lost a lot of blood, would probably pull through if the wound got treated.

The dogs seemed tame, so Jim figured there must be people around here somewhere. Putting the puppy in his saddle bag and securing him so he couldn't jump out, he then wrapped a blanket around the older dog and swung up into the saddle. Holding the dog with its head cradled in his left arm, he headed down the slope to what looked like a narrow road. The puppies black face sticking out of the saddlebag did look pretty comical and he had to chuckle at the innocent little face peering up at him.

Following the road, he thought about what had just happened. Some people would consider him a cold-blooded killer for what he had done, but he didn't feel that way. He had killed for the government, and everybody thought it was duty, glory and honor, even when most of those getting killed were just simple men with dreams of their loved ones and plans for their future.

Besides, what right did the government have to lay sole claim as to what was right or wrong...or when and how justice should be served? The government was supposed to be "made by the people...and for the people."

Since he was one of the "people", he felt comfortable

and confident enough to make his own decisions and deal with situations as they arose, not go running off to some bureaucrat and complain. Those two men were a social problem, and killing the scum had just made the world a little better place.

Unlike the typical murderer out west, or anywhere for that matter, Jim did not kill for the sake of killing. He reacted to situations by using common sense...backed up with a strong moral code. This outlook allowed him to be at peace with himself and sleep quite well at night.

About a half-mile up the road he saw a small town. As he got nearer he noticed a crudely painted sign welcoming people to Smithville. He hadn't heard of it before, but so many towns were springing up all over the place, with people moving in from back east, that he wasn't surprised.

Passing by a small wood frame house on the edge of town, a small girl and boy came running out, yelling at him. "Hey, mister, that's our dog you have."

Jim stopped. Smiling at the children standing by the road, he assured them if it was there dog, then he did indeed have it. "Is your pa around?" he asked, while looking at the general run down condition of the house and yard.

"Our pa died this spring," the tall gangly boy answered.

"I'll get ma," yelled the rambunctious little girl.

Moments later, a harried looking woman came outside, with another dog running and barking in front of her. Warily, she asked where the dog and puppy had been found and where the other ones were.

Jim briefly explained that some men had been shooting at them, and the little one with the black mask was

23

the only survivor, other than the older dog who needed to have a bullet wound taken care of. "I'm sorry kids, but there wasn't any more I could do," as he looked down at their sad, tear streaked faces.

The boy reached up to take the puppy. "Come here Tippy."

Looking at the small dog as he was taken out of the saddlebag, Jim didn't see any color spots that would give the dog a name like Tippy.

"Would you like to step down and bring Gus inside and we'll take a look at his wound?" she asked.

"No ma'am. The wound needs cleaned out and stitched up. Is there a Doctor in town?"

The woman paused, "there is a Doctor, a few buildings past the general store, but we have no money to pay him."

"That's okay," he assured her. "I'll take care of it and bring Gus back later."

Passing Smith's General Store, in the middle of town, he pulled up in front of a neat, and well maintained, two story house. The shingle out front read, "Dr. Stevens, General Practitioner." Carrying the dog as gently as possible, he went in and found the Doctor reading a journal.

"What have we got here," the Doc said, as he stood up and looked at the blood oozing out of the animal's hip.

"The dog belongs to a family living on the edge of town, and I came across him about a mile back." No need to tell the Doc all the details.

"I don't normally treat animals, but it's been slow around here lately, so I'll fix him right up. Who's going to pay for this, or will I get something in trade?" as he gave Jim a questioning look.

"I'll pay for him," as he flipped the Doctor a twenty dollar gold eagle.

"Hell, that's enough to get him a private nurse," the doc answered, as he deftly caught the coin.

Jim laughed, "Just fix Gus up and I'll be by later to get him."

Going back out into the bright sunshine, he thought about the widow and two kids trying to make a living out here. Thinking about it some more, he made a decision and headed for the general store. Entering, he noticed the fragrance of spices, molasses, and coffee all mixed with the smell of leather goods. It looked like a well stocked store. While browsing around, a man came up and asked if he could be helped. "Are you the owner?" Jim asked.

"Why, yes I am. My name is Joshua Smith...and the town is named after me," he said proudly.

"Figures," Jim mumbled.

"What was that you said, Mister?"

Jim looked around with a smile, "Oh, nothing. Anyway, you know the widow with the kids out on the end of town?"

"Sure do, they've had a real hard time making ends meet since her husband died this spring. Why do you want to know about them?"

Jim set down a small saddle pack he was carrying and pulled out 10 twenty dollar eagles. "I'd like to set up a store credit for them of $200 and get a receipt to take back to her. Also, would you put together a month's supply of all the basics you think a woman and two kids need and have it sent to them? I'll pay for those supplies separately."

Smith could hardly keep his eyes off the gold coins

25

as he stammered, "Whatever you say mister."

Laying down some money for the immediate supplies, Jim picked up four bottles of sarsaparilla and headed back to the Doc's place.

"I fixed the dog up as well as I could, considering the damage," the Doc said, as he led Jim back to the small operating room. "He needed the wound cleaned and a couple dozen stitches put in. He should recover just fine, other than he'll probably have a permanent limp. I only charged two bucks, so here's your change."

Jim picked up Gus. "It looks like a real nice job you did. I'll take him back out to his family, but you can keep the change. If someone else comes along and is short of money, remember this and cut them some slack."

The Doc laughed, "It's going to be hard forgetting about treating a dog and being paid in gold for it."

Carefully cradling Gus in his arms, he headed back to the woman's place. From a distance he could see the kids sitting on the front steps holding Tippy, with the female dog frantically sniffing her baby and looking around confused. He thought of these kids and their mother, having each other, the dogs, and a little shack they could call their own. It certainly wasn't what they had been expecting when they moved here, but a person had to make the best of what they had in this world and keep moving forward.

As he approached the yard, the kids looked up and ran over yelling, "Mom...mom, the stranger's back."

The mother came out wiping her hands off on an apron, and walked up to the horse. "Here, hand me Gus."

Jim transferred the dog down to the woman's arms and then dismounted. Leading Whisper over to a small tree and hitching him there, he pulled the bottles of sarsaparilla out of the saddle bag and walked back to where the mother and children were fussing over Gus. The female was excitedly sniffing her mate and trying to lick the bandage covering the wound.

The woman eyed him as he approached, "You know, for all you've done for us we haven't even introduced ourselves. My name is Sally, and these are my two children, Robert and Anna."

He took his hat off. "It's nice to finally have a name to go with you and your kids. My name is Jim McClair. The Doc said to bring Gus back if it looks like any inflammation starts to set in. Other than that he should be fine, all things considered. I also brought some sarsaparillas and thought we could visit for awhile before I have to get moving along." The way the kids were getting all excited, it had probably been awhile since Sally could splurge on something as simple as flavored soda water.

"That really wasn't necessary, but thanks. Let's sit on the porch and at least get out of the sun."

Settling down in a worn chair, he glanced over at the black masked puppy. "Where are the spots that would give him a name like Tippy?"

Sally seemed lost in thought for a moment and then smiled softly to herself. "Well, when Maggie had her litter, there were three male puppies. She paused with a sad look in her eyes and then brightened up. "Anyway, when the puppies were old enough to move about, the males would follow Gus around and learn how to mark their territory. That puppy would keep raising his leg higher and higher until he fell over on his back. It was the most hilarious thing you ever saw. So we named him

Tippy."

Jim laughed, "I would like to have seen that."

Just then, the kids came over and thanked him for the sarsaparillas. "That's okay kids. Glad you're enjoying them."

Anna shuffled her feet nervously and then looked up. "Those men won't come back and hurt the rest of our dogs, will they Mister McClair?"

He glanced over at Sally, who gave him a concerned look. "No Anna, I explained to them the error of their ways and they decided to move to a new frontier." The kids didn't need to know he had hastened their departure to the "new frontier" of hell.

Finishing his drink he turned back to Sally. "I was expecting to be in Helena this afternoon, but this delay means I'll be spending another night on the road. Before I head out, I wanted you to know that I opened up a $200 line of credit for you at the general store and here's the receipt," he said, while handing it over.

With a surprised and shocked look on her face, she exclaimed, "I couldn't accept this."

Pausing while he tried to figure out a way to phrase it, Jim finally said, "I'm not a wealthy man, Sally, but I have a steady income from some investments." He smiled, "you might say it came from a government grant, and besides, I've already done it so you might as well use it. The credit will let you and your kids get through the rest of this summer and next winter. By then you'll have decided whether to stay here and find work, or move on."

She considered it for a moment, "Since you put it that way, then I accept your generous gift."

Getting up, he patted Gus on the head, said his goodbyes and headed over to his horse. "Come on Whisper, it's time to get back on the trail." Mounting, he turned to leave when Anna and Robert came running up to him.

"Mister McClair! We wanted to thank you again for all you did for Gus and Tippy."

"I was glad to do it kids. If I had come along sooner, you'd have more of the other puppies also." Reaching down into his saddlebag, he observed, "Your mother is a proud, strong woman, and I think the three of you will do just fine no matter where you live. I know she doesn't like to accept charity, which is all fine and dandy to a point, so here's what I'm going to do. I'm giving each one of you a gold eagle. After I get down the road a ways, I want you to give them to your mother. Also, here's a dollar for each of you for a treat the next time you go to the store."

The kids looked up astonished. "Thank you, mister."

Tipping his hat to the kids and waving to Sally, who was still standing on the porch, he turned and headed back through town.

Several miles down the road he found a sheltered area that looked like a good place to stop for the night. Ground hitching his horse, he made a small campfire and rolled a smoke.

Thinking about Sally made him realize how he'd like to settle down with a woman. Having children wasn't something he really wanted, just someone to love and grow old with. With his steady income he could afford a small ranch, and enjoy it without worrying about whether he had a good year or not; like the problem facing so many ranchers.

Speaking of money, it was a good thing he would be in Helena tomorrow. After purchasing supplies and donating so much money to Sally back in Smithville, he was just about out of cash.

Luckily, Helena would have telegraph services so the banks there could confirm deposits in other banks farther east. Depending on what Wilson had in mind, he might have to withdraw more than usual.

The closer he got to meeting Wilson, the more he started to become curious why he had been sent for. Whatever it was, he would find out soon enough. After the coffee started boiling, he got out some jerked beef and had a simple meal before laying out his bedroll. While falling off to sleep, he thought about how pleasant and satisfying the day had turned out to be.

* * *

The first rays of light were just beginning to break the horizon when he got up. Stretching, he realized his muscles and bones took longer to bounce back from sleeping on the ground. Well, one more reason to find a good woman to live with...maybe a small ranch to call home. With that thought in mind, he saddled up Whisper and rinsed out the canteens, refilling them from the cold mountain creek he had camped by. Knowing he'd be in Helena by early afternoon, he decided to skip breakfast and instead just rolled a smoke for the start of his journey.

Traveling on the road was easy, but he could see that it generally followed the river. Coming to a low hill, he saw where the river made a huge sweeping curve, and decided to cut cross country. This would shave off a few miles and give Whisper a little more of a workout, while giving Jim a chance to see some different scenery in the foothills.

Turning his horse towards the lightly wooded hills, he began riding a course which should link back up with the river road in a mile or so. Losing sight of the road, he looked around at the total absence of signs of humans, and was thankful to let his mind enjoy the tranquility of nature.

The day looked like it would be a pleasant one, with a few light clouds floating across the sky. Glancing up, he could see an eagle or hawk; hard to tell from this distance, soaring majestically high up in the air. Yes, it couldn't get much better than this.

Shortly, Jim found himself coming back down a ridge where he could see the road once again. Sighing, he rode

Whisper back to it, continuing at a casual pace. Every so often there was a break in the foothills. If a person wanted to, they could easily travel up these canyons for exploration or maybe even find a nice place to homestead.

While passing the mouth of one of these breaks, he heard a pistol shot echoing down from the canyon. Wondering what it could be, he studied the grass leading into the canyon. He could tell several wagons had moved through here, probably a few days ago, because the grass was starting to grow back up in the wheel marks.

Since he had saved time taking a shortcut earlier, he decided to wander up the canyon and visit these travelers. Maybe they would know some information about the area that might be of use when he finally got around to talking with Wilson.

Following the same path the wagons had used was less work than cutting straight through the trees and shrubs, so he made good progress. He hadn't gone more than a quarter mile when he heard another pistol shot and faint screaming.

This was not good! Somebody was in trouble and might need his help. Spurring Whisper forward, he reached back and pulled out his Winchester. Levering a round into the chamber and putting the hammer on half-cock, he continued up the canyon.

Now he could hear the screams louder, and it sounded like women. From the different screams, it was definitely more than one.

Pulling his horse to a stop, he gave the situation more thought. He had no clue what lay ahead, and if he just galloped in, there might be some nasty surprise waiting.

Deciding he would make less noise on foot, he dismounted and led Whisper off into the trees. Tying a robber's slip knot, he patted his horse on the back and started out on foot. The slip knot was commonly used by criminals to make a quick get away. But it worked just as well to make sure if he couldn't get back for some reason, then the horse would eventually become thirsty and break loose on its' own.

He hadn't gone more than a couple hundred feet when he smelled tobacco smoke. Stepping behind an old gnarled tree, he looked carefully around. There! Back in a small cluster of trees, he saw a man leaned back against a tree trunk with a cigarette. Why would someone be casually smoking while there were gunshots and women screaming not much further up the canyon? This was beginning to look more like trouble with outlaws than Indians.

Moving farther back into the trees, Jim laid his rifle down and removed the big hunting knife he had strapped on his left hip. Quietly working his way through the trees, he snuck up on the man. He didn't have any intention of harming him, but the man was certainly behaving strangely, and Jim had no intention of committing a pilgrim mistake by casually calling out without knowing more about the situation.

Silently, Jim waited for the man to finish his smoke. After he had flicked the butt on the ground, the man stepped forward and looked up the canyon where the screams came from.

Jim took this opportunity to quickly take the last couple steps from where he had been hiding, and clamp a hand over the man's mouth. Pressing the tip of the knife against the small of the man's back, Jim whispered, "Don't make a move or ten inches of steel will slice through your heart." Feeling the strong grip around his head, and the point of something sharp through his clothes, the man froze.

Jim leaned closer and said quietly, "I'm going to take my hand off your mouth and ask some questions. If you try and yell or get away, then I'll kill you. Do you understand?" The man nodded his head.

Trembling, with a forearm around his neck and a knife in his back, the man asked, "What do you want, Mister?"

"I want to know who you are, and what the hell is going on up there. By the way, you're not a very good lookout."

Turning his head slightly toward Jim, the man started explaining. "My names Joe and our gang was heading towards Helena when we saw wagon tracks leaving the road and heading up this canyon. We followed the trail and discovered a small group of settlers. There were four wagons, several men, and about ten females camped out."

Getting a tight knot in his stomach, Jim prodded Joe with the tip of the knife. "Yeah, and then what happened?"

"We studied the situation, to make sure all the men were in camp, and then we opened fire. Most of the men were killed in the first volley, and after the smoke cleared a woman yelled to us that we could have the horses and wagons, just please stop attacking them. Our leader shouted to put down their weapons and the rest could live; all we wanted was any valuables they were carrying."

"I imagine the survivors believed you sorry sons of bitches."

Joe started to relax and get a little smug. "They sure did. One of the wounded men yelled to the women not to trust us, so Curly shot him. After that, the women threw down their rifles and pistols, and stepped away from the wagons. We went through the camp and finished off two men and a wounded woman. Once we were done ransacking the wagons and collecting all the valuables we could find, we proceeded to have some fun with the women. Then the boss sent me down here to make sure they got a warning if anyone came up the trail."

"One last question," Jim asked, trying to keep his anger down. "How many are in your gang?"

The man hesitated. Jim knew what the pause meant, and pressed the knife harder against the man's back. "You had better tell the truth."

Joe slowly let out his breath. "Okay, there are seven of us. Henry, who is our leader, Bo, Curly, James, Jane, Sue and myself."

Jim thought he had heard wrong, "You're telling me there are women in your gang?"

"We sure do, mister. I have to say they are two of the cruelest bitches I've ever come across. Just plain mean."

Contemplating what sounded like a vicious massacre, Jim realized if he wanted to save anybody that might still be alive he'd have to move fast.

With the story the outlaw had been telling, Jim had been gradually getting angrier…to the point of a killing rage. Swiftly bringing the knife up, he slashed it across the outlaw's throat. Blood gushed from the severed neck arteries and flowed down the front of Joe's shirt. While the body twitched convulsively, Jim lowered it to the ground. "Well, I guess there are only six of you now, you sorry piece of crap."

35

Going back for his rifle, Jim began sprinting up the trail, knowing full well the gang wouldn't feel the need to have a second sentry posted. Coming around a small bend in the road, he could make out the tops of the wagons over a low rise. He was now close enough so that, in among the screams, he could hear the laughter of the outlaws. One of the voices laughing was female. That had to be one of the outlaw women. Taking off his hat, he bellied up to the crest of the hill and slowly raised his head until he could survey the camp.

The settlers had picked a beautiful canyon to stop in. The place wasn't very big, maybe ten to fifteen acres. But what it lacked in size it made up for with a creek running through a stand of trees, and a small meadow with good grazing for the animals. It looked like a small slice of heaven and a good location for resting before continuing their journey. Then this scum came along and turned it into a living, and dying, version of hell.

Jim couldn't believe the carnage as he noticed dead bodies lying everywhere. He could see the outlaws standing around in a circle, where one of the outlaw women was kneeling by a female laying on the ground. He glanced over to where the other surviving women were clustered around the end of a wagon, and then shifted his eyes back to the outlaws.

Noticing all of the rifles had been leaned against wagons, and that their six-guns were holstered, he took a closer look at what was happening on the ground. He almost puked when he realized the outlaw woman was brutally assaulting the woman on the ground in a torturous and unspeakable manner.

Silently bringing his rifle into position, Jim thought about the "code of the west". One of the unwritten rules was that you were supposed to give a fair warning before you attacked someone, and another was that you were never supposed to shoot women.

Personally, he considered the code to be lacking in logic or common sense. You had to apply common sense to rules, guidelines, or even the written law, and consider the context of the situation you faced. Otherwise, a person might as well move back east where technicalities and ignorance seemed to go merrily along hand in hand.

And as far as a fair warning went, what was he supposed to do? Yell to the outlaws to stop what they were doing? All he'd get in return was a lot of gunfire and have absolutely no chance of saving any of the other women.

Taking another look at the abused woman, he could tell there was no way she was going to live. There was already a pool of blood around her from all the damage and she only appeared to be semi-conscious.

Quickly assessing the arrangement of the outlaws, he decided on the order of firing. First, he would take out the outlaw woman who was doing the assaulting. Hopefully, she would live long enough to suffer, and her victim would be aware of the turn of events before she also died and found peace in God's embrace. Next, he would shoot the man on the far left, and closest to the rifles. This would cause confusion right in the middle, where he would pour his remaining fire.

Wasting no time, now that he had made up his mind, Jim sighted on the woman outlaw and sent a bullet slamming into her. Not bothering to see what happened, he swung his rifle to the man on the left and dropped him with a round that shattered his breastplate, killing him instantly. Before the outlaws in the middle could figure

37

out what the hell had just happened to their fun, he emptied his bullet tube into them.

While the cloud of rifle smoke settled, he reloaded and then studied the camp. It appeared that no outlaws were still standing, and the surviving women were frozen in place; speechless and stunned by the sudden turn of events.

Jim rose to his feet and started down the slope. Keeping a close eye on the bodies of the outlaws, he shouted to the women that he was there to help and they would be safe now.

One of the women finally stirred and looked at him with a hopeful, yet frightened, look in her eyes. "There was another man with them. He's got to be around here somewhere."

Speaking softly, and with a soothing voice, he tried to calm her. "I've already met him and he's been waiting at the gates of hell fifteen minutes for his friends to arrive."

With that little exchange it seemed like a dike had broken. The remaining women began hugging each other and crying uncontrollably. Not knowing what to do, or say, he walked over to the outlaws and noticed one of the larger men was lying on top of another one, who looked like he was still alive.

Reaching down and removing their six-guns, he dragged the dead man off the bottom one. Sure enough, this one was alive and actually didn't even look like he had been hit. Either the impact of the larger man had knocked him unconscious or he was pretending to be dead and hoping he could somehow get away. Kicking the man in the ribs got an immediate reaction, so he had been playing possum. "Stand up on your feet, you sorry bastard," Jim said coldly.

Getting up, the outlaw asked, "Where the hell did you come from?"

Jim didn't bother responding. Turning his head to the women, he shouted, "It looks like one of your attackers lived."

At hearing this, the women froze for a moment and then started shouting. "Kill him! Kill the son of a bitch!"

With a horrified look on his face, the outlaw yelled, "You can't kill me! I've given up and you have to take me into town and turn me over to the Marshall. I know my rights!"

Jim shook his head in disbelief. "You're talking about rules of law after what your gang did to these peaceful people? You have some nerve. Did you hear that ladies? This piece of dirt wants to talk about his rights! I'll leave it up to you women, since you're the victims of this trash. Do you want me to take him to Helena, about fifteen miles away, or do we deal with justice right here and now?"

The women turned to each other and spoke in low voices for a few moments. Finally, one woman spoke up. "My name's Rachel, we've decided he should die as a token of vengeance for our dead companions and mates. Also, we want to be the ones to kill him."

He thought for a moment, "Well Rachel, you women have made a tough frontier decision, but I'll hang him myself. What you don't understand is that killing him yourself will make you feel good for a little while, but in the long run, it's an act that will haunt you the rest of your lives."

Hearing his death sentence announced, the outlaw made a leap for a revolver lying on the ground a few feet away. With one smooth motion, Jim drew his own .45

and fired. The bullet entered the right side of the man's head and blew a fist sized hole out the other side. As he thudded to the ground, Jim could hear a couple of the women vomiting at the gory scene. So they couldn't hear, he said softly, "Thanks for trying that. It was a lot easier on me than having to string you up. Though I wish you had suffered more."

While the women were consoling each other and wandering around the camp site mourning their dead, he built up the fire and put on a large pot of coffee. After cleaning and reloading his guns, he rolled a smoke and poured himself a cup. "There's hot coffee ready," he called out.

The women slowly straggled over and filled cups for themselves. An older one looked at him. "Mister, my nerves are shot. Would you mind rolling a smoke for me?"

"Be glad to." After rolling and lighting the cigarette for her, Jim introduced himself, but nobody seemed to be paying attention so he shut up.

After they had sat by the fire for a few minutes, he finally broke the silence. "We have to get these bodies buried."

Rachel glanced at him with a pained look on her face, "We'll get them ready for burial. What are you going to do about those murdering outlaws?"

"They don't deserve a decent burial, so I'll find a bank along the creek that I can just cave in on them. Then I'll start digging a large grave for your dead."

Walking back down the canyon to retrieve Whisper, Jim stopped and dragged the first outlaw he had killed out to the trail. On his way back, he tied a rope from the saddle horn to the legs of the dead man and dragged him

40

back up along the creek until he found a cut in the bank that should collapse fairly easy.

Leaving Joe's body there, Jim headed to the campsite and made repeated trips until he had all seven of the outlaws by the bank. Before he placed each body under the cut, he emptied their pockets of any money. The women would certainly need cash no matter where they went and it was only fitting the stolen money be used as partial restitution. When he got to the big man, he found a money belt. This must have been Henry, the leader. Jim counted the money and found over a thousand dollars.

The outlaws had plenty of money on them, so why did they have to go and attack these settlers? Shaking his head at the vicious senselessness of it all, he dropped the last outlaw on the pile. Climbing to the top of the bank, Jim took a shovel he had brought up on the last trip and gradually worked the soil. Finally, a large section of dirt fell, covering the bodies.

They weren't worth saying any words over, so he headed back to the camp where the five dead women lay on the ground wrapped in brightly colored blankets. The ones who had survived were standing around with blank expressions on their faces.

Surveying the tragic scene, Jim finally cleared his throat. "Excuse me. I'm going to go and dig one large grave. If you'd take care of any preparations for the men, then we could finish this depressing task." One of the women looked up with blood shot eyes and nodded, but didn't say anything, so he grabbed the shovel and went to find a suitable burial spot.

After the grave was ready, he carried the bodies over and asked if they wanted any special burial arrangement.

Gertrude, an older, thin woman with tears in her eyes,

41

spoke up, "We want the husbands with their wives laid next to each other and then the rest next to them."

Nodding, he began moving the bodies around where the women wanted them placed.

Two of the women had gone and picked armfuls of wild flowers that they distributed to the other women. After a few quiet moments for their own personal reflections, they tossed the flowers on top of their loved ones and friends.

When this was done, Rachel delivered a short prayer. "Dear Lord, we have no idea why you allow so much evil to exist in our midst. However, we believe you have a grand plan that transcends our earthly ability to understand. We thank you Lord, for sending Jim in our time of need to save us and for guiding his hand in the moments of retribution. We commend these souls into your loving care and ask for your blessing on those of us who remain. Amen."

One of the other women suggested singing, "Rock of Ages." Jim joined in, then started filling in the grave while the women began gathering small rocks to place on top of the dirt. This would at least keep animals from digging up the gravesite.

When they had all gathered back around the campfire, he looked at each of them. The simple act of burying their loved ones, and the physical work of collecting rocks for the grave, had apparently taken care of the emotional state of shock they had been in earlier. Trying to unwind, he listened to the women talking to each other about what they should do.

He finally interrupted, "Forgive me for being so direct, but we're only about three hours, by wagon, from Helena, but it's too late in the afternoon to head out today. What I suggest we do is transfer essentials onto two of the wagons. Then tomorrow morning we can hitch up the mules, tie the horses to the back of the wagons and be in town before noon."

Rachel, who seemed to have taken the role of leader, spoke up, "You're right. We can decide later what to do. Okay girls, let's stay busy and get the wagons loaded. Gertrude, would you mind making a Dutch oven stew while the rest of us prepare for the trip in the morning?"

Gertrude looked around with a blank look. "Sure Rachel and I'll also make some biscuits to go with it."

In the evening, with everything ready to go, they settled down to eat supper. Nobody's heart was really in it though, the girls just sort of picked at their food. Jim finally broke the silence. "Why did your group come into this canyon?"

Louise, a small but sturdy woman, spoke for the first time that afternoon. "We were headed to a ranching and farming community about fifty miles west of Helena that a friend had told us about last year. Anyway, one of the men, while scouting, rode up this canyon and said it would be a great place to rest up for a few days before heading into town and finishing the last leg of our trip. It was beautiful too, until those bastards showed up this morning!"

Feeling awkward about the sudden release of emotion, Jim hesitated and changed the subject. "I know it's going to be hard to sleep, but why don't you girls try and get some rest while I keep a lookout. If I can't stay awake, then one of you can spell me."

Nodding their heads in agreement, they started getting their beds ready while he refilled his cup and walked away from camp to have a smoke and give them some privacy.

Early the next morning, feeling exhausted from the last twenty four hours of stress and lack of sleep, he woke the women. While they were stirring, he added more water to the coffee grounds. "We'll be in Helena before too long, so let's just have some coffee and jerked beef for breakfast and hit the trail," he said. One of the women said it sounded fine, and nobody else said anything, so he went to hitch up the mules.

With everything loaded, and the women ready to head out, he stepped up into Whisper's saddle. "Let's get moving, ladies." It was a little slow going until they got down to the river road, but from there they made good time. They had left all the heavy furniture behind, which made a lighter load for the mules pulling, and they ended up seeing the outskirts of Helena in a little over three hours after leaving the canyon.

* * *

It had been years since Jim had been in this part of
the country and was surprised at how much the town had
grown. There were a lot more two story buildings, and
farther ahead he could even see a four story building
which was probably the hotel.

Bringing Whisper to a halt, Rachel who had been
driving the wagon behind him stopped also. "What is it,
Jim?"

Looking back at her, he replied, "I want a few words
with you ladies before we get into town. I think the first
thing to do is find a Doctor and let him take a look at
everyone. If you think you need it, he could give you
something to help take the edge off your pain and let you
get a good night's sleep." From the haggard, weary expressions on their faces, he knew most of them would
probably ask the Doctor for some sort of opiate.

Reaching into his saddlebag, he continued, "I know it
might sound kind of gruesome, but I took all the money I
could find on those outlaws. Figuring one of the reasons
they attacked your party was to rob you, I thought it fitting their stolen money should be used to help you get
back on your feet. It's almost two thousand dollars," he
said, while handing it over. "That should be enough to
take care of immediate needs and still have plenty left
over when you decide where you want to go from here."

Glancing back at the other women first, Rachel turned to Jim, "Speaking for me, and probably the other
girls, taking their money does sound pretty bad, and part
of me wants to throw it in a fire. However, you're right.
We need money and it will give us a small measure of
satisfaction using their ill gotten gains while they burn in

hell."

Nodding his head in approval, Jim smiled wryly. "You certainly cut right to the heart of the matter. Now let's go find the Doctor and then I'll go check into the hotel. It's probably that tall, brown with red trim, building over there. When you're through with the Doc, go there, and I'll have rooms already reserved for everyone."

Pulling up in front of the Doctor's house, Jim was astonished. The house was huge, a full two story home that must have five or six bedrooms on the top floor alone, judging from the number of windows he could see. The covered porch was at least ten feet deep and wrapped around all three sides of the ground floor. There must be a lot of sick and injured people coming here, he thought. "Well ladies, this Doc is either very good or he's the only one in town. You should be well taken care of here."

As he helped the women down from the wagon, each one took the time to hold his hand for a moment and thank him for everything he had done. "I'm glad I could help, and hopefully we'll see each other again at the hotel." Waving goodbye, he got on Whisper and headed into the downtown area.

Riding slowly toward the hotel, he studied the town and all the people scurrying every which way. Being the largest town in the area, and the seat of government, certainly brought a wide variety of people together, he thought. There were well dressed businessmen walking within several feet of buffalo hunters, who probably smelled worse than the animals they hunted.

Across the street was a fancy saloon with a second story balcony where the whore's could call down to men passing by. Standing above the men also allowed the women to creatively advertise their merchandise. At the same time, there were half a dozen women carrying signs declaring that drink and prostitution were the devil's work. Both groups pointedly ignored each other and he couldn't help but laugh out loud at the sight.

After reaching the hotel, he hitched Whisper to a rail. Taking his saddlebag and the long wooden case with him, he entered the lobby. Walking over to the registration desk, he leaned the case against it and set his saddle bag down. Shortly after ringing the bell, a well dressed young man came out.

"May I help you, Sir?"

"Yes, I'd like a room on the top floor, and facing the street if possible."

"There's one available, Sir. Would you please sign the register and I'll get your room key."

Glancing at the names written down while he signed his own, he noticed an entry; "Marjorie Clark". The date when she signed the book was several days ago. This was too much of a coincidence, so this had to be the Marge he had met briefly back at the train station. Oh well, he'd find out for sure later. Marge was apparently still here, and he would probably run into her in the restaurant or lobby one of these evenings.

"Here is your key to room 407, Sir," the clerk said, interrupting his thoughts of Marge.

"Do you have a hotel safe here?" Jim asked.

Checking the name that had been written in the register, the clerk looked up. "Yes we do, Mister McClair. What would you like to put in it?"

Picking up the wooden case, he handed it over to the clerk.

Placing the unusual case in the large safe, the clerk glanced at it curiously and then locked the door. As the clerk wrote out a receipt for the item, he asked, "Is there anything else we can help you with, Sir?"

Jim almost said no, but then remembered the women over at the doctor's office. "Yes, I'd like to reserve five rooms, on the same floor, for some women who should be coming here shortly."

The clerk checked his room chart. "We have enough rooms available on the third floor. Will that be okay?"

"That'll be fine."

"I hope your stay here is pleasant, Mister McClair."

"If nothing else, I'm sure it will be interesting," Jim replied, as he headed for the stairs.

Entering his room, Jim locked the door and placed his saddlebag on a chair. Taking out his colt, he removed a bullet and spun the cylinder so he wouldn't have a round under the hammer. No sense in accidentally firing off a shot. Besides, in town he should be okay without a full load.

Looking around the room, Jim noticed a small sign by a pull cord. Walking over, he read it. "Please pull on cord for room service." What would they think of next, he thought? Thinking about all the days he had been on the trail reminded him how dirty he felt, and probably looked. After pulling on the cord, he walked to the window and studied the street below him.

While he was watching the people, a sharp knock hit the door. Whirling, with the six-gun appearing in his hand, he asked, "Who's there?"

"You rang for room service, Sir?"

Sheepishly, he holstered his gun and went to the door. Damn, he was going to have to remember he was

48

in the middle of a town, not out in the wilderness where survival depended on quick reactions. Opening the door, he told the clerk he wanted a bath drawn.

"Yes Sir, the bath will be ready in about twenty minutes and will be in the room marked "Private" at the end of the hall."

"Thanks," Jim said, flipping the man two bits.

"Thank you, Sir!" the clerk said, grabbing the coin.

Removing a fairly clean shirt and pants from his saddlebag, Jim realized he had better find a place to get his clothes cleaned. Walking down the hallway, he was glad there had been a room on the top floor. It was so much quieter up here. He couldn't even hear any sounds from the lobby or restaurant below. After finding the door marked "Private", he opened it and stepped in the room. Hearing a scream, he jumped sideways into a crouch, drawing his gun and looking around.

There, standing in the middle of the room, was a tub with a woman in it taking a bath. She had stopped screaming at the sight of the gun, while he had frozen at seeing a woman in here. After a few seconds the shock wore off both of them.

"Jim? Jim McClair? Is that really you?"

Taking a closer look at her face, he was just as surprised to see Marge before him. "Yes, it's me," he said, with a suddenly dry feeling in his mouth and throat. "I'm sorry for intruding on you like this, I obviously made a mistake."

Marge slid a little further down into the water. "No, it's my fault. I forgot to lock the door, and that idiot clerk should have told you the bath for men is at the other end of the hall."

Mumbling under his breath, he turned to leave.

"Wait, Jim!"

Wondering what she wanted, and imagining all sorts of wonderful things, he paused and nervously asked, "Yes?" He had never seen someone blushing and smiling like the devil at the same time, but she managed to do both.

"I just wanted to tell you that Callie and I will be down in the dining room about eight o'clock tonight. You're welcome to join us."

"I'll think about it," he replied, as he quickly exited the room. Heading down to the other end of the hall, he suddenly realized it was a good thing he had left the room when he did. Just seeing Marge in the tub and thinking of her warm, naked body, soaking in hot sudsy water had started to make him hard. That would have been real embarrassing.

Jim finally finished his bath and went back to his room without seeing Marge, or anyone else. Putting his holster on and tying it down, he looked in the mirror and figured he'd better get a haircut and shave after dropping off his clothes. He also needed to let Wilson know he was in town and then find a store. The trail clothes he wore didn't look presentable enough for dinner with Marge and Callie in a hotel restaurant. Picking up the bundle of clothes, he locked the door and headed downstairs.

Stopping in the lobby, he waited until the clerk was free and then asked directions for someone who cleaned clothes.

"There's a Chinese woman that does the cleaning for the hotel and its' guests. If you'd like to leave them here, I'll have it sent out."

"Thanks," Jim said. "Oh, by the way, I need to find a

livery stable and also a bank."

The clerk thought for a moment, "The nearest stable is one block west of here and three blocks north. The biggest bank is the "Bank of Montana." It's across the street and up a block."

Turning to leave, Jim remembered Rachel and the other women. He turned back to the clerk, "Did several women check into those rooms I reserved?"

"They sure did, Mister McClair; about an hour ago. By the way, Mister McClair, the sheriff came by shortly after the women checked in and wanted to speak with you. I told him you were having a bath and he said he would look for you later."

The sheriff more than likely wanted his version of what had happened out in the canyon. He decided to go take care of his business and wait until the sheriff found him. Tipping the clerk a dollar for taking care of so much, he finally left the hotel.

Walking over to his horse, he rolled a smoke. Scratching Whisper behind the ears, Jim told him he'd soon have a comfortable stall to rest in and all the grain he wanted. Finishing his smoke, he mounted Whisper and followed the clerk's directions to the stable. The place looked well kept and clean, so he dismounted and went inside.

Sitting on a bale of hay was an old hostler, drinking a cup of coffee and smoking a pipe. Seeing someone walk through the doors, the man spoke up, "What can I do for you, mister?"

Jim looked around at the well ventilated stalls. "I need a place for my horse for a few days, maybe longer. You've got grain also, don't you?"

"Yup, I'll feed your horse two scoops of grain a day

51

for two bits and the horse will cost a dollar a day."

It sounded expensive, but the stable was close to the hotel, so he decided the price would be okay and led Whisper into a stall. Stripping the saddle and halter, he carried them and his rifle back to the old man. "I'll be leaving my rifle here. Will it be okay?"

"Sure, I'll put it in my sleeping quarters."

Jim could tell the old man was checking him out and seemed like he wanted to say something.

After a pause, the hostler said, "Word has it that some settlers were attacked outside town, along the old river road. I heard the survivors were escorted into town by a big man, on a horse that was described just like the one you ride. Pardon me for being nosy, but would you be that man?"

Jim sighed. Was he ever going to be able to just do something without having distractions? "Yes, I brought the survivors in, and they're staying at the Palace Hotel. Before you ask, the outlaws are all dead. Now, please just take good care of Whisper..."

"That's a mighty unusual name for a horse," the hostler interrupted.

"I gave him that name because he's quiet and likes to be left alone!" Jim said.

Seeing how annoyed the man was getting, the hostler quickly spoke up, "I'll take good care of your horse mister, don't worry."

Thanking him again, Jim stepped back out into the sunshine. As he made his way back to the hotel, he thought the day was turning out quite well. All he had left to do was get some money from the bank, get a haircut and let Wilson know he was in town. Later this afternoon he would also buy some new clothes.

Stepping up on the boardwalk along Main Street, Jim paused to look at all the activity. It seemed like everyone had places to go and business to conduct. Walking casually up the street, he found the bank where the hotel clerk said it would be.

Entering the large, quiet lobby, he was impressed at the expensive detailing and design that had gone into the construction of the bank. Obviously, the owners expected it to be here a long time. Hearing someone clearing their throat and saying, "Sir," Jim turned around and saw a well dressed bank teller looking at him.

"Sir, may I help you over here?"

Jim walked over to the teller. "I sure hope so. Short of robbing this place, how do I withdraw money?"

Nervously eyeing him, and looking at the tied down gun, the teller hoped the man was joking about the robbery part. "I'm not sure what you mean, Sir?"

"Sorry," Jim said. "I didn't explain myself very well. What I meant was, I have funds available in other banks farther east and south of here, and I need to have access to them."

Breathing a sigh of relief, the teller explained he would have to talk to the Bank President. "I'll go let him know someone is here to see him. May I ask what your name is?"

"Jim McClair."

The teller returned shortly from a rear office. "The president should be with you in a few minutes. If you care to relax while you're waiting, there are some comfortable chairs over in the corner by the window."

While Jim was resting in one, he noticed Rachel

entering the bank and called over to her.

"Oh, there you are Jim. We were wondering if we would see you again."

"I'll be around for several days," Jim said. "What brings you in here?"

"After talking about things, we decided that I should open an account and deposit most of the money in it. We don't have any family to go back to, so we plan to buy, or set up some business here in Helena and try to make a go of it."

He smiled at her take charge attitude. "I'm sure if anyone can make a business succeed, it's you."

Smiling at the compliment, she changed the subject. "When the sheriff heard about us, he came and asked about what happened out on the river road. He didn't seem real pleased about you killing those women outlaws. He sounded like you should have somehow taken them into custody and brought them in. He also seemed bothered that you took the money from the outlaws and gave it to us."

Jim shook his head at the apparent stupidity of the sheriff. "The hotel clerk already mentioned he wants to talk to me. Thanks for tipping me off about his attitude."

Just then the teller came up and told Jim the president would see him. "I've got to go, Rachel. But if there's anything else you girls need help with, just come and ask. I'm in room 407."

"Thanks, Jim. I'll see you later."

Ushering him into the President's office, the teller announced, "Mr. Dunfree. This is Mister Jim McClair."

When the two of them were alone, the bank president motioned for Jim to take a chair. "How may I help you, Mister McClair?"

Looking at the huge oak desk, the plush carpeting, and thinking about the expensive bank lobby, he wondered how there was any money left to even help people. "Just call me Jim. My problem is that I have money in other banks and I need to find a way to get some of it."

"Well, Mister...I mean, Jim. That creates a difficulty for us as well. You see, we're large enough to have reciprocal arrangements with some of the other big banks, but we would need to wire them for a description of you. This protects both you and the banks. However, the telegraph wires have been cut to the east of us, and without some positive identification we are unable to simply hand over money on your word alone."

Realizing the truth and sense of what the banker said, he replied, "I understand your position. Would a letter from John Wilson satisfy you?"

The banker looked surprised, "You mean, the Territorial Governor?"

Jim nodded.

The banker looked at Jim with new interest. "I'm going to be at his place for a dinner party tonight, I can ask him about you. Why don't you come back in the morning, and I'm sure we will be able to take care of your business then."

Jim stood up to shake the bankers hand, "That'll be fine. See you in the morning."

Walking back out into the open air, he put his hat back on and wondered what he should do next. Deciding to get a haircut and shave first, and then let Wilson know he was in town, he stopped a businessman on the street. "Excuse me, could you tell me where a barber is and how to get to the Capitol Building?"

Looking at Jim's appearance, the man smiled and

nodded. "There's a barber shop just past the saloon. You can't miss the red and white striped pole out front. As far as the capitol building, you have to go east four blocks and then head north about a half mile. You'll spot it real easy once you get away from these buildings."

Thanking the man, Jim walked up the street to find the barber shop.

Hearing the bell on the door jingle as it was opened, the barber got up from the chair where he had been reading a dime novel about violent men in the west. Seeing Jim walk in, the barber got excited. This man was big, as far as most men went. He had a tied down gun and the friendly smile belied the coldness in his ice-blue eyes. Dusting off the chair, the barber asked, "What can I do for you today, Sir?"

Jim looked around at the empty shop, "I'd like a short haircut and a shave."

Watching as the man sat down, the barber noticed he slipped the thong off his colt and loosened it in the holster. Sweet Jesus, this was one dangerous or paranoid person the barber thought, as he wrapped a towel around the man's neck.

Trying to strike up a conversation, while he began cutting Jim's hair, the barber asked, "Did you hear about the group of settlers that were attacked out along the river road?"

"Yes, the first person who told me about it was the hostler where I stabled my horse."

Trimming around the ears, the barber kept talking. "The way I hear it, some gunfighter came along and wiped out the entire outlaw gang…faced them all down at the same time!"

Smiling at how the story had gotten exaggerated by

people who weren't even there, Jim replied, "Only a fool would have taken on a gang of armed men and women face to face."

Deciding the man wasn't going to get into the spirit of the story, the barber became silent and started lathering up his face. When the shave was almost over, the door bell jingled and Jim tightened his grip on the colt underneath the apron. He relaxed when he saw the man had a star pinned to his coat.

Taking a look around the shop; the sheriff spoke up, "From the description of the hotel clerk, you must be Jim McClair. I'd like to hear what happened out there with the settlers. Apparently you eliminated the entire Bitterroot gang."

Good God, the barber panicked, here I've been trying to tell the story to the very man who killed the whole gang. Nervously wiping the rest of the lather off Jim's face, he said, "That will be one dollar, Mister."

Glancing in a mirror before responding to the sheriff, Jim got a dollar out, "You did a nice job. Here's two bits for a tip."

"Thanks, Mister," the barber said, as he stepped quickly back into a corner.

He turned to the sheriff, "Yes, I'm Jim McClair, and I was the one who helped those ladies. But I got there after the gang had already killed the men, and some of the women, after raping and torturing them."

"That's basically what Rachel told me also," the sheriff answered back. "Also, I understand you took the money from all of the outlaws and gave it to the survivors, and that you killed two female outlaws. The money should have been turned over to the sheriff's office and I don't understand why you had to shoot them instead of bringing them in for trial? Killing women isn't taken real lightly out here."

Contemplating the greed and lack of common sense the sheriff was demonstrating, Jim decided to talk about the money first. "Why should I have turned it over to the sheriff's office?"

"Because the money was stolen, we would have held onto it in case someone showed up to claim it," the sheriff said piously.

"You know that's not true," Jim shot back. "From what I saw of the gang, they didn't exactly leave a trail of survivors to wander back in search of their stolen money. What you really wanted was to hang onto it for awhile, and then you could keep it for yourself or turn it over to the city treasurer. I gave those women that money and they'll keep it! The money is small enough compensation as it is, considering what they've been through and had done to their loved ones."

Realizing that topic was going nowhere fast, the sheriff changed the subject. "What about those female outlaws? Couldn't you have brought them back alive?"

If the situation hadn't been so tragic, Jim would have laughed at the idiocy of the sheriff. "What those female outlaws were doing sheriff, was worse than anything I can remember ever seeing a man do!"

"But still," the sheriff continued, "they were women."

Plainly getting irritated at the dense sheriff, Jim fired back, "What do you think the victims were?" Sensing from the look in the sheriff's eyes that a little common sense was starting to seep into his brain, he asked, "Tell me sheriff, have you ever killed a rabid dog?"

Puzzled by the question, he said, "Sure, probably

have to shoot one, maybe two rabid dogs a year out here. What's that got to do with anything?"

Jim pressed on, "Before you shot them, did you check to see whether they were male or female dogs that had gone rabid?"

"Hell No! I got them in my sights and...," realizing the simple trap he had fallen into, the sheriff tightened his jaw. "You can't compare people with animals."

"You're right! Comparing that scum with dogs isn't fair to the animals."

Knowing the point Jim had made was true, but feeling frustrated at losing control of the situation, he said, "Maybe what I should do, Mister McClair, is take you down to the jail and see if there are any "wanted" posters on you?"

Jim stood there calmly, and said softly, "You could try."

The sheriff bristled with anger, "Are you threatening a law officer?"

Jim stared him down, "No! You're threatening me and I'll defend myself if I have to. I won't draw first, but I don't have time to listen to your bullshit. So make up your mind what you want to do, because unless you have something worthwhile to talk about, I need to let the governor know I'm in town."

Speechless at the turn of events, the sheriff stood there with a blank look on his face as Jim put on his hat and walked out the door. Turning, the sheriff was about to ask the barber what the hell had just happened, but noticed he was already heading out the back door.

"Well! Isn't this just going to sound great down at the saloon," he said out loud to an empty room. "To hell with it, I'm taking the rest of the day off."

Following the directions he had been given earlier, Jim made his way towards the Capitol building. Once it was in sight, he stopped by the river and rolled a smoke. Enjoying the moment, he watched a couple of young boys fishing from the bank. Remembering how much he had enjoyed the lazy, carefree days of his own childhood, he walked over and asked how they were doing.

"We're doing alright, mister," the smaller freckled faced kid piped up. "Look at these trout we caught," he bragged, as the other kid pulled a line out of the water.

Sure enough, there were half a dozen nice trout; the big one must have been close to twenty inches long. The smaller ones were beautiful also, and would look even better in a frying pan. He could almost taste the fried fish, rolled in flour and cooked in some grease until the skin was crispy. Finishing his smoke, he told the kids to have fun and continued on his way...fishing and a fresh trout dinner occupying his thoughts.

Pausing at the open gates, Jim studied the Capitol building and admired the well manicured grounds. He was also impressed with several fancy carriages parked along the driveway. Walking up to the entrance, he was met by a deputy who appeared to be more for show than any serious protection.

"Can I help you, Mister?" After Jim presented the telegram from the governor, the deputy said, "Just go up the main stairs and hang a right. You can't miss his office."

Thanking the deputy, Jim walked down the hallway and climbed the stairs. Even on a hot summer day, the building was cool because of all the stone work. It felt refreshing. Entering an office fancy enough to be the governors, he saw a man sitting at a desk working on some papers. Jim rapped his knuckles on the door, "Excuse me, I'm trying to find the governor's office."

Pausing from his paperwork, the man glanced up and felt an instant dislike for Jim. He had worked for the governor for three years now, and people still treated him like a doorstop. Then a man like this walks into the office; tall, good looking, exuding confidence, and casually acting as if the governor was his equal! God, how he wished he was more like these men! Someday he would have money and power, and he would make sure everyone knew who was important.

Keeping those thoughts to himself, he smiled, "I'm the governor's assistant and behind me is his office. May I help you?" After Jim showed the telegram again, the assistant said, "The governor is with someone now, he should be through in ten minutes or so, and then I'll let him know you're here. You can just wait over there in a chair if you'd like."

Nodding, Jim sat down in a surprisingly comfortable chair and started leafing through a magazine. Getting bored with the articles, he pulled out the makings for a smoke and started rolling.

Hearing the paper rustle, the assistant looked up with an air of disgust. "Would you mind not smoking in here, Sir?"

Pausing, Jim glanced up. God, the man reminded him of a weasel. Reading the nameplate on the desk, he said, "As a matter of fact I do mind, Mr. Hartman. It's going to be a cold day in hell when a man can't come into a public building and enjoy a smoke. So I suggest you open a window, go back to your papers and shut the hell up!"

Taken aback by the hostile tone, Mr. Hartman shrank down in his chair and pretended Jim wasn't there.

Minutes later, Jim could hear voices approaching the closed governor's door. Standing up as the door opened, he was pleasantly surprised to see Marge exit first, followed closely by Wilson.

"We'll continue this talk later Marge, after I have- Jim! Stepping past Marge, Wilson eagerly grabbed his hand and started shaking it. I was beginning to wonder if you were going to show up at all. Marge told me she had seen you at the hotel."

Shifting his eyes to her, Jim saw a red flush creeping up her face. "I had to take care of a few errands first, John."

Wilson caught the eye movement and noticed Marge blushing, and wondered just what had happened back at the hotel.

"Anyway," Wilson continued, "I was just telling Marge I would get back to her after I had a chance to talk to you, but I have a meeting in the conference room that I need to get to right now. How about I swing by your room around ten o'clock tonight and bring you up to date, while we bullshit about old times?"

"That's fine with me. I've been invited to join Marge and Callie for dinner at eight, and we should be done by then."

Looking Jim up and down, Wilson commented, "I can't believe how well you've held up. Other than filling out a little more, you look just the same as the last time I saw you."

Jim laughed, "I wish my body felt as well as you say it looks."

After Wilson left, Marge and Jim looked at each other for a moment. "Well, I guess I had better head back to town," he said to her, "It's a long walk."

"You walked all the way from the hotel?"

Jim explained how he had wanted to stretch his legs and it really was a very pleasant stroll.

She shook her head, "I have a buggy out front, why don't you ride back with me?"

He smiled at his good fortune, "I'd love to."

As they walked out to the front of the building, he couldn't help but admire the way she carried herself. She had a fine figure, and the gingham dress she was wearing accented her hips and cleavage...Stop it Jim, he told himself. Getting his mind off those distracting thoughts, he asked, "What did Wilson need to discuss with you after he talked with me?"

Knowing this wasn't the time to go into details, she hesitated, "I think I should leave most of it to John for an explanation." Looking up at him, she smiled, "What I will tell you, though, is I'm actually an undercover Pinkerton agent. Wilson sent for me several weeks ago and I traveled out here with Callie. Besides being a friend, she's also my assistant."

Speechless, and shocked to say the least, he finally blurted out, "A Pinkerton agent?"

She laughed at the look on his face, "Yes, a Pinkerton. Is that so hard to believe?"

Fumbling for words, he finally told her he didn't expect to find a woman so attractive, and feminine, working as a detective.

"Thank you for the compliment, but what did you expect a female agent to look like?"

Now it was his turn to blush, "I don't know. I never

really thought about it, but I sure wasn't expecting one to look like you!"

As they got into the buggy, she said, "We can talk about things later. For now, I want to get back to my room and relax for awhile before getting ready for dinner.

Riding back to town was uneventful...and quiet. He was still trying to sort out that Marge, who he had been lusting after, was a Pinkerton agent! Up until now, he hadn't been concerned about talking with Wilson, but what problem did Wilson have that would also require a detective? He would get answers tonight though, so he might as well enjoy her company now. By the time he got his thoughts straightened out, they were approaching the hotel and as he helped Marge down from the buggy, he told her he was looking forward to dinner with her and Callie.

"We'll have a table towards the back of the restaurant," she said.

"I'll see you then," he replied. Tipping his hat, he turned and walked up the street. He normally didn't drink much, but with everything that had just happened he decided to stop at the saloon and have a beer.

Entering the saloon, he stepped to the side and studied the people. There was a card game going on at a table against the wall and two bored looking prostitutes sitting at a far table, talking low and polishing their fingernails. Up against the bar were four men listening to the barber describe how Jim had made the sheriff back down. The story had changed so much that it sounded like he had pistol whipped the sheriff into submission. Seeing no sign of a threat, he walked over to the vacant end of the bar and motioned the bartender for a beer.

Glancing over to see who had come in, the barber froze in mid sentence.

Smiling, Jim raised his beer in a salute and told the barber to continue. "Just don't come over here asking any fool questions." The man nodded, and went back to telling his story, in a much lower voice however.

Rolling a smoke, he realized one of the men at the card game was watching him. Not making eye contact, because he really didn't want trouble, Jim lit his cigarette and took a long swallow of beer.

Suddenly, a booming voice came across the floor, "I hear you're the low down skunk that shot up the gang out along the river road? A couple of those boys were friends of mine. What do you think of that, Mister?"

Knowing there was nothing else to do, Jim turned to face the table. The man who was speaking had a typical surly expression on his face. He wondered how so many of these cretins were still alive. You would think someone would have killed them off, but they kept cropping up like bad weeds.

Jim pondered the man's question, "Well, if they were your friends, then what I think is that it's too bad you weren't out there with them." The man stood up, he was even bigger than Jim.

"What's that supposed to mean?"

Quietly, Jim replied, "Because then you would be rotting out there with them, instead of in here bothering me."

Slamming back a shot of whiskey for courage, the man challenged Jim, "I'm not armed and you wouldn't be talking like that if you didn't have a gun strapped on."

Thinking how convenient it would be to just shoot the son of a bitch, Jim held back. Taking off his gun belt

65

and handing it over to the barkeep, he turned back. "If you think guns are what give me strength, then come on over and let's get it on!"

Even though he was bigger than Jim, the man hesitated because of the calm, casual way, he had handed his guns over to the barkeep.

"Come on, Bill," yelled another man at the table. "Teach the stranger a lesson! Go over there and kick the shit out of him."

Egged on by his friends, and booze, the man approached. When he was within a few feet, he suddenly bellowed and charged. It would have worked against an inexperienced fighter, but Jim was prepared. He knew if he had frozen, the man would have smashed his back into the bar railing. That, by itself, might have seriously hurt him. If nothing else he would have been pinned against the bar where the man could have used his larger size to pound away at Jim's face and body. Luckily, he knew these crude tactics and stepped aside at the last moment.

Quickly reaching out, Jim grabbed the back of the man's coat and helped propel his head into the side of the bar. Bottles and glasses bounced, rattled, and broke with the impact. Backing up, Jim waited for the man to stumble to his feet.

"I damn near cracked my head, you bastard." With a little more caution this time, the big man approached Jim.

Wanting to end this quickly, because he had no desire to impress strangers with how long he could fight, Jim took up a classic fighter's pose and motioned for Bill to come at him.

Putting up his own arms, Bill gave Jim an ugly smile,

"Let's see what you have to say after I connect one of my fists against your face."

Jim shrugged slightly, "Do what you think you can."

Enraged, the man edged in, trying to get close enough so Jim would have no room to swing.

Instead of backing up, Jim stepped quickly forward to close the gap and feinted with his left fist and Bill swung his forearm up to block it. When he did, Jim put all the speed and strength he had into his right fist, and cut underneath the man's arm. Slashing up through the opening, his fist connected with Bill's throat.

There was a sudden silence, as the sickening crunch of cartilage told everybody in the bar that the man's windpipe had been crushed. The big man grabbed at his throat and began gagging for air as he collapsed to the floor. Someone yelled for a Doctor, but he was already turning blue and probably wouldn't last long enough for help to arrive.

Walking back to the bar to get his gun, Jim heard another chair scrape against the floor.

"You just killed Bill! He was my friend, you son of a bitch."

Whirling around and going into a crouch, Jim mentally kicked himself for handing his gun over to the bartender and tried to decide the best way to get out of the man's line of fire. Suddenly, the twin hammers of a shotgun being cocked back made everyone freeze. Standing by the end of the bar was the barkeep. The shotgun barrels looked like small cannons and Jim was grateful they were pointed at the other man.

"Red, you get that gun back in your holster. I don't know who this stranger is, but Bill has been talking all last night and today what he would do if he ever found the person who killed Henry. Well, Bill found him, and was even given a chance to fight without guns, so I'll not stand by and let you shoot an unarmed man."

Reluctantly, Red holstered his gun and went over to Bill's body. Kneeling, Red said something about getting even another time and then left the saloon.

Putting away the shotgun, the bartender smiled, "that beer and another one are on the house, Mister," as he handed over Jim's gun and holster. The Bitterroot gang has been roaming this neck of the woods for years. It's about time someone caught them flatfooted."

Thanking the bartender for the beer and the timely intervention with the shotgun, Jim pulled out the makings for a smoke.

"Here, Mister, have one of these cigars I keep back here."

"Thanks."

Just then, two deputies came in. "What the hell is going on in here? The barber came running down the street, yelling someone had been killed."

The bartender walked around the bar and gave the dead man a nudge with his foot. "Bill was prodding this man," as he pointed at Jim, "and the stranger took off his gun and let Bill have a chance to fight with his fists. The fight only lasted about a minute before this man killed Bill with a blow to the throat. It was clearly self defense," the bartender added.

Thinking about it, they looked at Jim, and then glanced at each other. One of the deputies stated, "From the description the sheriff gave, before he took the day off, you must be Jim McClair. The strange thing was, we were told to leave you alone, unless you went crazy and started shooting up the town."

Jim gave the men a faint smile, "Well, I really wasn't planning on doing that today, so right after I finish my cigar and beer, I'm heading back to the hotel."

Turning back to his drink, he listened to the bartender and deputies arguing about who was responsible for removing the body. Reflecting on how fast things could change in life, he finished the beer and headed for the batwing doors.

As he reached them, one of the deputies spoke up, "Watch out for Red, Mister McClair. We've never caught him, but he has a reputation as a back shooter."

Thanking the deputy for the warning, Jim stepped out onto the boardwalk. Adjusting his hat to cut down on the late afternoon sun hitting his eyes, he remembered he had forgotten about getting some new clothes. Looking up and down the street, he saw what appeared to be a general store a few buildings away and headed for it.

Entering the store brought back fond memories of when he was a child and his folks would take him along when they had shopping to do. Back east, stores had gotten so big that they carried specialized merchandise. However, out in the west the general stores still carried everything imaginable. The smell of leather goods intermingled with the scents of spices and molasses...the air almost had a tangible taste to it.

Wandering over to the clothes section, he found a nice fitting black vest. He also selected a red shirt with a white tie, and a pair of black pants.

As Jim purchased the items with his dwindling supply of money, he realized there was only enough left for dinner tonight and breakfast in the morning. But since there wasn't anything more he could do about it today, he headed back to the hotel with pleasant thoughts of dining with two beautiful women.

Nodding to the clerk as he entered, Jim climbed the stairs and went to his room without seeing anyone. After locking the door, he put his clothes down, and checked the time on a cheap clock sitting on the dresser. He still had a couple hours before dinner, and after such a full day he decided he had better get some sleep.

Waking up feeling refreshed, he glanced over at the clock and realized he had slept longer than he wanted to. It was almost seven thirty, and dinner was supposed to be in a half hour. He had better hurry.

Putting on the new clothes felt good. He adjusted the shirt and vest and then made a loose knot with the tie. Once, a woman had showed him how to tie a fancy knot, but he could never remember how to do it right, so he just fluffed the tie up and made it look like it belonged. Strapping on his holster, he checked his gun and headed downstairs to the dining area.

As Jim was entering the restaurant, a waitress came up and told him, "We would prefer that people not bring firearms into the dining area."

He looked at her with a bemused smile on his face, "Thank you for letting me know what your preference is. I have my own preference, and that's to carry my gun when, and where I feel like. So, if you will kindly take me to Marge Clark's table, I would appreciate it."

Starting to open her mouth, the waitress stopped when she saw the cold intensity in his eyes. Shrugging, and thinking she didn't get paid enough to enforce management rules, she said, "Please follow me, Sir."

The waitress took him back to a table in the rear, where Marge and Callie were enjoying a glass of wine and giggling. As he approached, they looked up and stopped talking.

"Jim! Glad you could make it for dinner. You remember Callie, don't you?"

He took his hat off, "I sure do, pleasure seeing you again, Callie. I see you girls have already started on wine."

Lifting the bottle, Marge gave it a gentle shake, "Well, this one is almost empty. Would you like to share another bottle with us?"

Thinking about wine and food together wasn't real appetizing, so he shook his head, "I'll just have a shot of whiskey and a beer."

Marge motioned with her hand and a waitress headed over to the table.

Callie held up the empty bottle of wine, "We'd like another one of these and Jim would like a shot of whiskey and a beer."

"I'll have the bartender send them over right away. Would the three of you like to order now?"

Glancing at the other two for approval, Marge nodded, "I'd like a steak, medium well, mashed potatoes with gravy and whatever vegetable you have available."

Having already looked at the menu, Callie ordered, "I'll have the same as Marge, except I'd like the chicken instead of steak." As Jim prepared to order, she interrupted, "Let me guess. You want potatoes and a rare steak, with no vegetables, right?"

He laughed, "That's what I want. You sure like to give me a hard time though, don't you Callie?"

She laughed, "Someone should, and it doesn't look like Marge will. Besides, it seems to me you enjoy the attention."

After the waitress left, and their drinks had been

brought over, the three of them settled in to enjoy each others company and relaxing conversation.

All too soon, the food was in front of them and they all dug in with a healthy appetite. It was a real treat to eat a well prepared steak again. Jim relished the wonderful smell, flavor, and tenderness of the meat. Eating food he cooked on the trail was enjoyable because he liked the solitude, but having all these people around was a small price to pay as he savored every bite of the excellent beef. Noticing the women were enjoying their food as much as he was, he paused and raised his glass, "I'd like to propose a toast to fine food and beautiful women." Marge and Callie both laughed, and raised their wine glasses to join the toast.

When their meal was done, and the waitress had removed the plates, Marge asked, "Are you going to have any dessert, Jim?"

He leaned back, "I never thought about dessert. I just figured I'd have another beer. Why, what do they have?"

"They have this really wonderful treat," Callie said. "The chef takes two cookies and places a slab of icecream in between. You have to try it. You can't just keep sucking down beers."

Smiling, he turned to Marge, "Is she this blunt with everyone?"

Marge laughed, "Not really, but Callie seems to have it in for you though, doesn't she?"

"Alright, Callie, I'll give your fancy dessert a try."

He usually didn't care for sweets, but he had to admit the cookies with ice-cream was a pretty tasty novelty. As he was finishing the dessert, he looked across the table at Marge and thought how beautiful she was. The happy relaxed expression on her face warmed his heart. While he was thinking about his feelings for her, she picked up a napkin and began dabbing at the melted ice cream dripping on her fingers.

"You know the only problem with these," she said, "is the ice cream melts so fast that it drips all over the place."

As a drop fell on her breast, he leaned over without thinking and offered to wipe it off with his napkin. Pausing, as he realized his indiscretion, Marge blushed and mumbled something about doing it herself.

Callie almost dropped her glass when she heard his offer. Damn, here's this attractive man making a comment like that, and Marge just gets a mischievous, embarrassed look in her eyes. Hell, she might as well go back to her room now and find a book to read.

Before he could think of something to say, a booming voice broke the awkward silence. "There you are, Jim!"

Everyone looked up as John Wilson walked to the table. "I finally got away from that boring dinner party and hurried over here to see you. It looks like you had more enjoyable dinner companions than I did," he said, while admiring the two women.

Sliding his chair back, Jim stood up and shook Wilson's hand. "Glad you made it down here. We were just finishing dessert."

"That's right," Marge added, "we were just talking about *dessert*!"

Ignoring her emphasis on the word, he kept talking to John. "Why don't we go into the bar and catch up on old times, and I'm curious to find out what made you send for me?"

"Sounds like a good idea, Jim. If you ladies will excuse us, we have a lot to talk about." Turning to Marge,

Wilson added, "I presume we will continue our discussion tomorrow?"

"Yes, why don't I come to your office about noon and we can have lunch at the same time," she replied.

Jim stood there, fumbling with his hat, "I want to thank you and Callie for inviting me to dinner. I had a wonderful time."

His interest in Marge was so obvious, Callie couldn't resist, "I'm sure the pleasure was all hers, Jim."

As they headed for the bar, he heard Marge saying something to Callie, and then they both burst out laughing.

Sitting down at a table in a quiet corner of the bar, he thanked Wilson for his great timing.

"What do you mean?"

"Well, we haven't seen each other in years, and just when I was trying to recover from putting my foot in my mouth, you walked up and took care of the situation."

"What did you say?" Wilson asked.

"Nothing really, I was deep in thought about Marge, and said something before giving it a second thought."

Laughing, Wilson slapped the table with his hand, "So the reclusive Jim McClair has feelings for Marjorie Clark! She is one attractive woman, isn't she? Has a good head on those beautiful shoulders too. Do you want me to tell Marge how you feel about her?"

Jim smiled, "That's okay, John. I think I can handle it on my own."

After two beers had been brought over, they talked for a while about what each had been doing during the years since the war. Finally getting around to the present, Jim asked, "What's this I hear about Marge being a Pinkerton? You've got my curiosity up! You send for me, and a detective at the same time. What's going on?"

Wilson held up his hand to slow him down. "Whoa. I'll answer all your questions, but let's take them one at a time."

Realizing they had all night to talk, if need be, Jim relaxed and pulled out the makings for a smoke. "You're right, John. Start where you want to."

"Let me give you some background first, Jim. Over the years, while working towards becoming the Territorial Governor, I've made several investments.

One of them is a mining concern about seventy miles from here, next to the small town of Deer Creek. I own a 25% share of the mine, and its' been a steady producer for myself and the other owners. The mine presses the extracted gold into crude bars, and twice a year brings a heavily guarded shipment to Helena, where it's then sent by rail to a mint. Once it gets on the train, it's the railroads responsibility to safeguard the gold.

We've never had a problem with a shipment from the mines to Helena. Oh, once in a while some gang will try an attack, but they never succeed. That's because Mike Johansen, the lead driver, is also one of the owners, and you can imagine how strongly the shipments are defended. I should mention," Wilson added, "the other two owners are Brad and Jason Johansen. Brad oversees operations and Jason is the mine engineer.

Anyway, last summer, several gold bars were found missing from the inventory. At first, the owners thought it was internal theft and instituted security measures. Simple ones; like carefully checking any people or wagons leaving the facilities. This seemed to take care of the problem. Several weeks went by and there were no further thefts.

However, when the last shipment of the summer reached Helena, and the boxes were opened up for railroad security to confirm the number of bars and weight, we had a nasty surprise. Three of the boxes had been packed with an equivalent weight of iron."

Jim interrupted, "How much gold has been taken so far?"

Wilson thought for a moment, "Each box holds 12 ten pound bars. So we lost 360 pounds of gold, which at current value comes to almost a hundred thousand dollars."

Jim leaned back and took a drag off his smoke, "By wagon that must be a three or four day trip. Did they stop anyplace where the switch could have occurred?"

"No! Southwest of here there aren't any towns between Deer Creek and Helena. There's only a way station where the men can rest the horses for the night. When they do stop, there are three guards posted at all times, and besides, when the boxes were opened, the original issue padlocks were still in place."

So, Jim mused, "The switch had to occur back at the mining facilities. Was there anyway to tell if the most recent boxes had been the ones switched?"

"No, the boxes aren't numbered by date of loading. Once a box is filled, Brad or Jason will confirm the count, personally place the padlock on the box and then stamp the box with the mining logo. The boxes are then placed in a basement room located in the mine headquarters. A guard sits upstairs in a locked office and only the mine owners have access to the keys which unlock any of the doors."

Jim shook his head, "I can't believe somebody managed to bypass that level of security without anyone knowing. At least it explains why you brought in a Pinkerton detective. But I don't know anything about unraveling mysteries, so why did you send for me?"

As John paused before continuing, the bartender walked up, "It's getting late, Mr. Wilson, is there anything else I can get the two of you?"

"Yes. You could bring us a bottle of your finest bourbon and a pitcher of beer." Waiting until their order was brought back, they smoked in comfortable silence. When the bartender brought their drinks back, Wilson told him,

"Since we're the only ones left in here, why don't you put the closed sign on the door and go home."

Nodding, the bartender smiled gratefully, "Thank you, Sir."

After he left, Jim asked again, "So, why did you send for me?"

"I'll bring you up to date on the gold first. The mining and crude refining continue year-round, but no shipments are sent during the winter because of the harsh weather. This spring, when the first shipment was scheduled, the boxes were opened up before loading and four more boxes were found with iron in them instead of gold. The Johansen brothers were just about ready to shoot everyone at the mine, they were so angry." Wilson chuckled, "I don't think even the Territorial Governor could have covered up an incident like that."

"How soon did you find out about it?" Jim asked.

"Within hours I had a telegram informing me of the theft."

"I thought there have been problems with the telegraph lines?"

"We have a lot of difficulties with lines being cut east of Helena, mostly renegade Indians and the occasional outlaw. The army tries to keep the lines up, but it takes time to find the cut and do the repairs. But for some reason, we've never had a problem with the lines to Deer Creek."

"However, getting back to our concerns and why I asked you to come out here; someone has been shooting cowboys, farmers working out in the fields and even an occasional miner wandering in the valley."

Jim held up his hand, "You mean like in gunfights, or bushwhacking?"

Wilson shook his head, "No, I should have clarified what I meant. What we have is a long distance shooter …a sniper!" He paused to let Jim digest this information. "What I need," he continued, "is a person I can trust who understands the mind of a sniper."

Now it makes sense, Jim thought. "So, what you need," he said slowly, "is for me to go in, locate and terminate this sniper, while Marge figures out how the gold was switched and where it went to?"

"Exactly, but it goes beyond that," Wilson said. "I don't even know if the two events are related. What I do know, is that whoever is behind the gold theft is very smart and patient. Furthermore, bushwhackers can be hired for a few dollars, but you know better than I do that a sniper is a highly skilled professional. Whoever hired him must also have a lot of money and patience. That's why I have a gut feeling there's a connection."

Wilson took a sip of whiskey, "In the last two months there have been seventeen confirmed shootings. Also, between last year and this year, the mine is missing over three hundred thousand dollars in gold.

Yes, I want you to find the sniper. But even more important, I want you and Marge to find out who the brains are behind this operation and bring him in for trial. I know it's going to be dangerous, but I remembered how pissed off you'd get when innocent people, or animals were hurt. Now that you know why I sent the telegram, what do you think?"

"It's going to be dangerous," Jim stated. "A good sniper can hit targets close to a mile away, depending on conditions. If he's shooting from that far away, then even if you immediately know where the shot came from, by the time you get there, the shooter will be long gone. It does make me angry though, to think one person could terrorize an entire valley, whatever the motive might be."

"I just thought of another question about the gold, John. If someone figured out a way to switch the gold with iron, then why just stop at a few boxes? Why not switch it all?"

"That's a good question. We don't know. The only thing we can think of is that the people responsible thought we wouldn't find out again until the railroad checked the contents. They probably hoped there would be doubt as to where the switch occurred," Wilson finished.

"That theory makes sense," Jim said.

While John poured two shots of whiskey, Jim filled their beer glasses again. He rolled another smoke, and commented, "The whole situation sounds intriguing and pretty strange, but since I can't do anything until I get to Deer Creek, is there anything else you could tell me about Marge? All I see when I look at her is a beautiful, alluring woman."

Wilson lit a cigar and exhaled, "You've been around. Surely you've seen lots of pretty women."

Jim smiled, "Yeah, but there's something about her that makes me think of more than just lust."

Wilson laughed, "Well, you certainly have a way with words, don't you? Marge comes from back east, which you already knew. What you don't know is that I knew her family, and the last time I saw Marge she was attending a finishing school for young ladies."

Jim interrupted, "How the hell did she go from that to a Pinkerton?"

"Let me tell you the rest, Jim. After school, she married a young banker. Everybody thought they had an ideal marriage, but several years later there were still no children, and then one day the bank was robbed and her husband was killed in a shootout. Marge was despondent for months and then her grief turned to anger."

After taking another sip of his whiskey, he continued, "She wanted to get even with criminals and other low life scum, so she hired a retired soldier to teach her everything about firearms. Then Marge used her father's influence to get hired by the Pinkerton Agency.

With her drive, ambition, and knowledge of weapons, the agency soon had her working undercover. For example, if there was an area plagued by unsolved crimes, Marge would move in, keeping her eyes and ears open for information.

Most men would see a young, pretty woman and talk in front of her, or brag about their exploits. Soon she would know the people involved and who was in charge. Then the Pinkerton's would come down in full force and clean up. Apparently, Marge is quite intuitive when it comes to solving crimes."

Jim sat enthralled, "It sounds like a person could write a book about her adventures."

"Maybe a writer will someday," laughed Wilson. "Anyway, when the whole problem with the missing gold started back up again this year, I contacted the Pinkerton Agency and told them I wanted her for a job I had. They argued with me about sending a woman out west, but I told them it was Marge or nobody. The agency didn't want to lose a governor as a client, so here she is. That pretty much sums up why she's out here and why I asked you to help out," Wilson concluded.

*   *   *

Groaning, Jim rolled over in bed. It sure had been fun at the time, talking with John and reliving some of their past, but now he remembered why he didn't drink very much anymore. He was getting too old to stay out all night and then try and function the next day. Not only was the drinking hard on him, but his body took more time to recover than it used to.

He was glad he had answered the telegram, however. Hunting a sniper would certainly challenge his abilities and the thought of going cross country with Marge was an offer he couldn't refuse.

Looking at the clock, he was shocked to see it was already going on two o'clock in the afternoon. He lay back down and tried to remember if he was supposed to do anything today. That's right. He had to get money from the bank.

He rolled out of bed and stumbled to the wash basin. Splashing water on his face, he then wet down his hair, and got dressed in his regular jeans and shirt. Buckling on the gun belt, he stepped into the hallway. Grateful no one was around, not the way he felt, he headed for the stairs.

Walking down the street to the bank refreshed Jim considerably, so by the time he got there, he was ready to actually talk to someone. Entering the bank, he saw the same teller at the cage. "Excuse me," Jim said. "I was supposed to come back today to arrange a withdrawal."

Recognizing Mister McClair from the day before, the teller said, "I'll let Mr. Dunfree know you have arrived, Sir. If you would just a wait a moment, he'll be right out."

Jim barely had time to start looking around the bank when he heard his name called. Turning, he saw Mr. Dunfree waving him over.

Jim couldn't believe the difference in Mr. Dunfree's attitude. Whatever Wilson had said must have been pretty good, because the banker pumped his hand like a long lost friend and offered him a cigar.

"No thank you. I had my fill of tobacco last night."

Sitting back down in his chair, the banker said, "Please, call me Alex. At the dinner party with John Wilson last night, I asked about you. I must say, Jim, you certainly are in the good graces of the governor. He told me to advance you any amount of money you asked for, and he would personally guarantee it. So, how much money would you like to withdraw? Five hundred, a thousand, what did you have in mind?"

Jim's mind went blank for a moment. He couldn't believe Wilson had been so generous, and this was before he even knew if Jim would accept the job. "I think one thousand dollars will be enough for now," he finally replied. "If you could give me half of it in gold eagles and the rest in paper, I would appreciate it."

"No problem at all, Jim. No problem at all. If you would just stay here, I'll go to the vault and get your money. While you're waiting, would you please sign this paper acknowledging receipt of it?"

The banker returned shortly with the coins placed in a leather pouch and the currency in an envelope. Thanking him for everything, Jim prepared to leave.

"Oh, by the way, Jim, as long as you're in town you won't have to worry about carrying the money around. The sheriff was told to have his deputies keep a discreet eye on you."

He didn't really need anyone watching over him, but it was a nice gesture. "Thanks for letting me know," Jim said, as he shook the banker's hand and left.

Leaving the bank, he looked up and down the street. Sure enough, there was a deputy lounging by a store window across the street. Smiling to himself, he slung the leather pouch over his shoulder and headed back to the hotel where he found John waiting in the lobby.

"Hi Jim, I've just finished a late lunch with Marge and thought I would come over and tell you the general plan we came up with. Should we go into the bar?"

Jim shuddered at the thought of alcohol, "That's fine, but let's stick to coffee today."

Wilson laughed, "The hair of the dog was a little too much, eh?"

"Something like that."

Finding a corner table in the bar, they sat down and ordered coffee. Wilson paused, and took a sip before starting. "We decided the two of you should go in as husband and wife. The cover story will be that you're interested in investing in the mine. This will give you an excuse to have private meetings with Brad and Jason. Obviously, you'll let them know the real reason for your coming out there.

This will also take care of the gossip, and people won't wonder why the two of you are riding around the valley. Hopefully, one of you will notice something that doesn't quite fit and figure out what's going on."

Jim thought for a moment, "It sounds good to me. The plan is simple, so we won't be trying to make up some elaborate story that can unravel. There are a couple of things I'll need though."

"Name it."

"First, I'll need a much more powerful set of field glasses than the one I carry. Second, I think it would make sense if I was deputized in case things start going haywire."

"Neither one of those will be a problem, Jim. The surveyors for the railroad use very strong telescopes for their long distance measuring. I can have one of those delivered here to the hotel. I'll also send a letter over that identifies you as a special deputy for the Territorial Governor. Will that do?"

Jim nodded, "Perfect. Oh! By the way, I want to thank you for what you did with the bank president."

Wilson smiled, "I was pleased to do it. If you hadn't taken control of events back during the war, neither one of us would probably be sitting here now."

"When did Marge want to get started?" Jim asked, changing the subject. He had never felt bad about what had happened, but he didn't want to discuss it either.

Wilson shrugged his shoulders, "She's ready to go anytime you are."

Jim thought a moment, "There isn't anything else I need to do in town, so we could leave first thing in the morning. Marge will need a horse, though."

"I'll pick out a good one for her from my personal stock," Wilson replied. "Well, that settles it then," as he stood up. "If you need anything, you can wire me and I'll help you anyway I can." Shaking hands, they wished each other good luck.

After Wilson left, Jim decided he really needed to get a good nights sleep. Finishing off the last of his coffee, he went back to his room and sprawled across the bed. The sounds of people and traffic kept him awake for awhile, but eventually he got into the rhythm of the background noise and fell into a deep sleep.

Drifting in and out of a restful slumber, he heard a gentle rapping at the door. Quickly picking up his gun, he asked who was there.

"It's me, Jim."

Glancing at the clock, he saw that it was almost ten o'clock. What was she doing, knocking on his door this late? Setting his gun down, he walked over and opened the door. Standing there, looking as pretty as ever, was Marge with a covered plate in her hand. Checking out the hallway, and not seeing anyone else, he invited her in. "What brings you up here this time of night?"

With a devilish smile that he liked so much, she said, "I brought up some cookies and ice cream. I thought you might like to have this tonight instead of whiskey and beer."

The offer took him by surprise, "Yeah. That does sound good. Here, have a seat."

Giving Jim one of the desserts, she sat down and began eating her own. After a few minutes of comfortable silence, she glanced down, "Look what I've done now! Ice-cream has dripped off my fingers and onto my dress. What will I do now?" she lamented with an impish grin on her face.

Damn, Jim thought. What would the western code of conduct call for in this situation? Rapidly sifting through possible answers, he finally said the one thought that kept popping back into his head. "Would you like me to lick the ice-cream off?" Smiling, she set her plate down on the dresser.

With the first rays of daylight coming through the window, Jim stirred. Starting to turn over, he realized

86

Marge was snuggled into the crook of his arm. Looking down at her breathing gently against his chest brought back pleasant memories of last night. Damn, she had been a little tiger once she got going. Suddenly realizing he had better get up before he disturbed her; he carefully moved her arm from across his stomach, and edged out of bed.

Jim did his best to dress quietly, but Marge heard him and rolled over to ask what he was doing. As she fluffed up the pillow, the blanket slid down and he could see her large firm breasts.

"Good morning, Marge. I'm sorry I woke you, I was just going down to get an early breakfast." Trying to keep from staring at her body, he asked if she wanted to join him.

"No thank you, it won't be a good morning until about noon. Why don't you come back to bed instead?" she asked languidly.

"Believe me, I would love to," he said, in a husky voice, "but after breakfast, I need to get Whisper from the stable."

"Well, come back and wake me in a few hours," as she rolled back over and pulled the blankets up around her head.

Taking one last look at her, he sighed and left the room, quietly closing the door behind him. Walking into the restaurant, he was surprised to see Callie sitting at a table having breakfast. Walking over, he asked if he could join her.

Hearing Jim's voice, she looked up with a smile on her face, "Please do, but I'm surprised you have the energy to get up this early."

With a straight face, he replied, "I feel on top of the

world this morning."

She snickered, "I'll bet you felt on top of the world all night."

After a little friendly bantering, he sat down and ordered some eggs and a steak."

Waiting for the food to arrive, he asked her what she would be doing when they headed out later in the morning.

"John Wilson invited me to stay at his mansion," Callie replied. "Even though I won't be going with the two of you, I'm still Marge's assistant and will be receiving reports from her. Besides, John is a really nice man. Also, I found out he's a widower, so we'll see what happens."

Jim laughed at the obvious plan, "Good luck, Callie, he's a good man to ride the river with." After she left and he was done eating, he started rolling a smoke to enjoy with another cup of coffee. Just as he lit up, the hotel clerk came in carrying a small rectangular wooden box.

"There you are, Mister McClair. I thought I saw you come in here earlier. A messenger from Mr. Wilson delivered this box and a letter for you first thing this morning."

Thanking the clerk, he tipped him two bits and opened the envelope. The letter had the official Montana Territorial Seal on it, and said that Jim McClair was a duly appointed special deputy for the Governor. The letter went on to describe his physical appearance and directed all law enforcement officers in the territory to follow any orders he might have to make in the course of his inquires. Jesus! This had the stamp of a lawyer all over it.

Folding up the letter and placing it inside his vest, he

88

slid the box over and opened it. He could tell it was a telescope, but it sure didn't look like the kind he was used to. This must be the instrument Wilson said the surveyors used.

Lying in the bottom of the box was a short tripod. Setting it up on the table, he could see it originally had longer legs. At least Wilson knew his business. He had had someone cut the legs off, so when the telescope was mounted on the tripod a person could lie on the ground and study the terrain while keeping his own head just inches off the ground.

Satisfied with the letter and telescope, he paid for breakfast and went back to the lobby. Handing the clerk the box, Jim asked him to hold onto it while he went down to the stable.

Walking down the street towards the livery stable, he was admiring the peaceful morning when he saw some kids laughing and running up the street towards him. About half a block ahead the kids darted into an alley.

Just when he was starting to remember the carefree days of childhood, the kids ran back out. The only difference was that the children were no longer laughing or yelling. Slowing his pace, Jim thought about it. If the kids had seen a dead body or something else gory, there would have been some screaming or morbid curiosity. But these kids had run out of the alley with fear on their faces.

Taking the thong off his gun, Jim came to a stop at the edge of the alley. Peering around the corner, he saw a man about 15 feet back. It looked like the one who had threatened to get even with him for killing Bill at the saloon yesterday. He seemed to remember someone calling him "Red." Getting really pissed off that his good mood had been ruined, he shouted, "Hey, Red! Is that you?"

The man yelled back, "Yeah! And I told you yesterday I'd get even. I've been keeping an eye on the hotel and when I saw you heading in this direction, I figured you must be getting your horse."

Jim sighed, "I suppose you're armed?"

"No," Red snorted sarcastically, "I thought I'd just call you names when you walked by and maybe throw a rock at you."

Jim's patience was running real low. "Get out here in the street and let's finish this now!" Red slowly walked to the mouth of the alley with his hand hovering near the butt of his gun.

"Don't worry, Red, I'm not going to draw unexpectedly. Just come out in the street and we'll square off, man to man." As Jim watched, Red stepped back-wards until they were about thirty feet apart.

Thinking of all the gunfights he had watched or been involved in, Jim reflected on one common theme. Speed went hand in hand with accuracy. Over the years several men had been faster on the draw than him, but their shot had gone wild. Some men, if given time to shoot, were considerably more accurate than he was, but in the life or death tension of a gun fight simply could not clear leather fast enough.

Jim had also seen gunfighters who combined a level of speed and accuracy that would have put him six feet under. Fortunately, those gunslingers were like him, they wanted to be left alone. Red, on the other hand, had a sleazy backstabbing look about him, and Jim knew he preferred to shoot his victims from the shadows.

Red finally stopped and stared at him. After a few seconds, Jim asked impatiently, "Are you going to draw?"

Red began to sweat a little, "I was just thinking that maybe I didn't want to kill you today."

Jim got a cold look in his eyes, "You don't understand, Red. If I hadn't been warned by you scaring those kids out of the alley, your ambush might have worked. It's way too late for second thoughts now. I'm giving you the chance to draw first, but if you try and turn your back to me, I won't hesitate to shoot. I'm not going to spend any time worrying about you trying to ambush me some other time."

Nervously, Red stood there trying to figure out a way to get an edge on Jim. The only thing he could think of was to start talking and draw in the middle of saying something.

As Red started speaking, Jim watched his eyes closely. While Red was asking if they just couldn't forget the whole thing, his eyes shifted slightly and Jim knew Red was going to draw. Red didn't even get his gun clear of leather before a .45 slug from Jim's gun slammed into his chest with the energy of a sledgehammer. The blow sent Red flying back several feet before his body hit the ground.

Keeping an eye on the dead man while he replaced the spent round, Jim could hear doors opening and people shouting. The sound of running feet caught his attention and he spun around with his gun leveled. It was one of the deputies he had seen yesterday.

The deputy came to a stop, panting heavily. "Mister McClair, are you alright? I'm sorry I wasn't watching you, but I didn't get on duty until eight o'clock, and when I got to the hotel the clerk told me you had already left. I was wondering where to find you when I heard a shot."

An old man yelled from a nearby house, "What are you worried about him for? He shot a man! Arrest him!"

The deputy looked at the old man with disgust, "Shut up, Clyde. You know damn well you didn't look out the door until after the fight was over, so you have no clue what happened."

Rambling on about too much violence in the city, and nobody doing anything to stop it, Clyde turned and slammed the door.

Now that people were going back inside, the deputy looked down at the body and asked, "Red did promise to avenge Bill's death, didn't he?"

Jim nodded, "Well, it did work out for the best."

The deputy looked up, "How do you mean?"

"Now they're together again."

The deputy chuckled, "I guess you're right, though drinking beer together was probably a lot more pleasant than what they're doing now."

Jim helped drag the dead man back to the edge of the alley. Straightening up, he told the deputy he needed to get his horse and head back to the hotel.

"Do you mind if I tag along with you?" the deputy asked. "It would be a lot easier than following you from fifty feet back."

"That's fine with me."

As they walked along, the deputy asked Jim where he was going when he left town.

"I'm heading over to the mines at Deer Creek. I've been thinking of investing in the Johansen Mine Works and maybe buying a small ranch in that area."

The deputy sounded wistful, "I sure wish I could do something exciting like that. No matter how big Helena gets, I'll never be more than just a deputy."

"Don't be too hard on yourself," Jim encouraged. "You have a good job, and with Helena growing the way it is there are a lot of opportunities available to a steady man like yourself."

Nodding in half-hearted agreement, the deputy stopped suddenly, "Wait a minute, did you say Deer Creek a moment ago?"

"Yeah, why do you ask?"

"Well," the deputy said, "There have been a lot of killings in Deer Creek Valley this year. In fact, no new settlers have headed in that direction this summer because of the trouble in that area."

As they approached the stable, Jim replied, "Well, I'll at least take a look around."

Entering the stable, the deputy went over to talk to the hostler while Jim walked over to Whisper. "How have you been doing, boy? Have you missed me? You're looking well rested. Are you ready for a ride?" Whisper excitedly started prancing in place. "Come on, boy, let's get you saddled up."

After getting Whisper ready for traveling, he led the horse out front and then went back to get his bedroll and Winchester. As he walked up, the deputy and the hostler stopped talking. He smiled to himself. No doubt, they had been talking about the shooting. "What do I owe for my horse?" Jim asked.

"Nothing, you already gave me enough up front to cover everything."

Reaching into his pocket, Jim pulled out a dollar. "This is for taking good care of my horse."

"Why, thank you, Mister."

Standing by Whisper, he told the deputy he would be

riding back to the hotel and could probably make it that far without protection.

The deputy smiled, "Try and keep a low profile when you ride past alleys."

Laughing, Jim mounted his horse and rode back to the hotel. Hitching Whisper to a rail out front, he noticed a beautiful Appaloosa tied to the post. He hadn't noticed the horse when he left this morning and wondered who had arrived.

Entering the lobby, he asked the clerk who the horse belonged to.

"An employee of Mr. Wilson brought it over a few minutes ago. He said it was for Marge Clark. Though I don't know where she plans on riding around here."

"I'll be riding with her," Jim said. "We'll both be checking out this morning. Could you get the bill in order while I see if she's ready?"

"Be glad to, Mister McClair."

Quietly entering his room, he found Marge was already gone. Looking around, he realized the new set of clothes he had bought was the only thing left to pack. Folding the clothes as neatly as he could, he squeezed them into his saddlebag and walked down the hall to Marge's room.

As he knocked on her door, he could hear women talking. When the door opened, he was taken by surprise. Marge was standing there in men's jeans and a thick cotton shirt. He couldn't help noticing she filled out the jeans a whole lot different than men did. Blushing at the obvious path his eyes had taken, he looked up.

Marge was smiling, "Do I look ready to ride, Jim?"

Yeah, that and a whole lot more, he thought. "The clothes are certainly practical, I'm just not used to seeing a woman dressed in jeans...at least not looking like you do."

Now it was her turn to blush. Changing the subject, she said, "I was just saying goodbye to Callie and telling her to expect telegrams on a regular basis."

After he told Callie goodbye, and to have fun getting to know Wilson better, Marge and he went down to the lobby. After paying the bill, he asked the clerk to bring his box from the vault.

"Yes Sir, Mister McClair," the clerk said, as he went back and opened the vault. Bringing the long wooden case out front, he set it on the desk.

Curious, Marge asked, "What's in the case?"

Jim made sure the small lock on the case had not been tampered with, and then glanced over at her, "Just a personal belonging."

Judging by the slight shift in his voice when he answered, she decided not to pursue the question.

"Don't forget this small box Mr. Wilson sent over," the clerk said, as he placed it on the desk.

"Thanks for reminding me. My mind seems to be wandering these last couple days." Picking up both cases, he turned and asked if she was ready.

"Ready as I'll ever be. Let's get started."

* * *

When they were several miles outside of town, she asked how long it would take to get to Deer Creek.

"If we were going through rough country," Jim explained, "we would probably need a week to get there. However, with the road that the shippers use we can make good time. I figure we'll have two nights on the road, and be there sometime on the third day."

"That's not too bad," she replied. "This is beautiful scenery, and as much as I like a warm bed, it's good to get away from people."

He was surprised that she felt the same way he did about towns and people. As the miles disappeared, they talked of interests and places they had been. Jim knew this was a personal question and none of his business, but he had to ask. "Wilson told me you never had children. Didn't you want any kids?"

Marge was thoughtful for a moment. It really wasn't any of his business, but it seemed so natural to open up to him. "Yes, I wanted a family and we had a baby on the way, but then I had a miscarriage. The doctor told me something had gone wrong and I would never be able to have children."

Now Jim was embarrassed he had even asked. Since the cat was out of the bag, however, he continued on. "Did you ever think of getting married again after your husband was killed?"

"I thought about it, but the ones I was interested in wanted to have a family and that wasn't something I could provide. I've dated men, but nothing serious. How about you? You're middle aged, attractive, and seem financially secure. You also seem to have a way with

96

women. What's your story?"

"Actually, not much different than yours. I've known a few women over the years and I thought one relationship would end in marriage. However, the more we got to know each other, the more I realized she wanted to move to a large city and have children. As much as I like kids, I don't want any of my own. It's kind of ironic, isn't it? You can't have children and I don't want any."

She smiled, "Maybe Wilson is playing matchmaker and this was his way of seeing if we liked each other?"

Enjoying the thought of spending years with Marge, he laughed, "I would hope he could have come up with a less dangerous plan to get us together. I'm going to try and track a sniper, and you're supposed to find out what happened to nearly half a ton of gold bars. My mission is straight up deadly, and if you get close to solving your mystery then I'm sure whoever is behind it will be just as violent in trying to keep the gold."

"You're right about that, but since we won't even know where to start until we're there and can look around and ask questions, why don't we just enjoy this time alone? By the way, how far do you want to travel today?"

"Let's keep riding until a couple hours before dusk, and then the first good place we find we'll make camp."

"That sounds fine to me."

The miles drifted past without seeing any other travelers and the afternoon was gorgeous, with only a slight breeze blowing in from the north. Jim had always enjoyed riding the trails alone, but having Marge with him seemed to make the journey complete.

Giving their horses a chance to exercise and break up the routine at the same time, they would gallop for a quarter mile, then trot for awhile, and finally, walk the horses for a mile or so. This method worked well, and allowed them to cover long distances without tiring the horses out too much. Every so often, they would also stop by a creek and stretch their legs while the horses drank and grazed the rich grass growing by the water.

Judging from the increasing length of their shadows, Jim decided they had better keep an eye out for a decent campsite. "We've made pretty good time so far," he told her. "I figure we must have covered about twenty five miles. No sense in driving ourselves too hard on the first day, right?"

"I could sure use a rest," Marge said, as she arched her back. "It's been quite awhile since I've ridden on a horse for this many miles."

Riding along, while keeping an eye out for a camp-site, she thought about Jim. I wonder what it would be like to settle down with a man like him. He's let me know he doesn't like living in a city, but he seemed to enjoy staying at the hotel. Blushing, she remembered their last night in the hotel. That could certainly explain why he enjoyed his stay. There were so many questions she wanted to ask him. He appeared to be a walking con-tradiction. Take those eyes for example. If you got past the cold hardness of them and looked deeper, you could see a kindness that was rare in a man.

Noticing her flushed face; he asked if everything was okay.

"I'm fine. I was just thinking how nice a campfire and a cup of coffee would be."

"There's a low rise over there," he said, pointing to a spot about a mile ahead. "Since we're going to be stop-ping for the night anyway, let's race."

"You're on," Marge yelled, as she took off her hat and slapped her horse on the flank. Shouting and laughing, they urged their horses on. She had a head start due to her quick reaction to his challenge. But Whisper gradually overtook her horse and by the time they hit the crest of the hill he had beaten her by two or three horse lengths.

Halting, they dismounted to let the horses catch their breath. While they walked the horses slowly down the other side of the hill, he commented, "You certainly don't ride like a city girl."

"I might have been raised in the city, but my heart has always been in the wilds of nature. When I had weekends off from the boarding school, I would go to my uncle's farm in the country. There he would let me ride to my hearts content.

In exchange, I helped with milking and feeding the cows, sometimes with canning fruit and vegetables. It was hard work, but at the end of the day I was exhausted and would fall into a wonderful sleep, dreaming of where I would ride the next day. When I got married those visits stopped, but the memories are still there. Anyway, that's where I learned to ride and take care of horses."

He stopped in the middle of the road. "Those sound like some peaceful and innocent days. Memories like those can go a long way toward helping a person through rough times."

"Amen to that," she agreed.

Deciding the horses had rested enough; they mounted and began a steady walk down the road. Looking around as the horses plodded along, he pointed, "Hey! Look down the road. Doesn't that appear to be buildings a couple miles away?"

She held up her hand to shield the sun from her eyes, and squinted, "It does. Probably the way station Wilson told us about."

"Should we just stay there tonight?" he asked. "I know it's not the same as camping out alone, but we might as well take advantage of it."

"That's probably a good idea. Oh, that reminds me. Since we're going to start meeting people, we need to decide on our last name."

"What do you mean?"

She chided him, "If we're supposed to be pretending to be man and wife, then we have to use the same last name."

He conceded the point, "Do you want me to use "Clark" or do you want to use "McClair"?"

"Well, I'm used to working undercover." Seeing the twinkle in his eyes, she laughed, "No, I didn't mean that! What I meant was, I can remember to use your name easier than you will mine. Besides, "Marge McClair" has a nice ring to it."

Oh great, he thought, is she using the word "ring" for some subtle hint, or is it just an expression she happened to use. "That will be fine, Mrs. McClair."

She smiled coyly, "Come on. Let's ride down there and get these horses unsaddled and in the corral, so we can go in and have some food. I'm famished after riding most of the day."

Kneeing their horses into a canter, they rode the rest of the way in companionable silence. Arriving at the small way station, they were greeted by a man of about forty. Standing by his side was a teenage boy. Both were looking at them with surprise on their faces. Glancing at

100

Marge, Jim shrugged his shoulders.

Turning back to the man, he asked, "Can we get a meal here and a place to sleep for the night? Also, we'd like to put our horses in the corral?"

"Sure can, Mister. The boy will take the horses and you can come on in. My wife is fixing dinner now. The only place to sleep though is on some hay in the barn, or in a lean-to out back."

Dismounting, Marge slid her Winchester out of the saddle scabbard and started walking towards the house.

"Do you really think you need that?" Jim asked.

Turning, she replied, "I don't carry a six gun like you do, and I'll be damned if I'll ever put myself in a defenseless position." With that, she headed into the house.

The owner of the way station chuckled, "Other than a little unnecessary profanity, she got you there, Mister."

Scratching his head at the idea of independent women, Jim agreed. Reaching out his hand, he said, "My name is Jim McClair, and that's my wife, Marge."

The man brought his own hand up, "Pleased to meet you, Jim. My name is Ralph, my boy is Terry and my wife, Cindy, is in the house preparing a hot meal. Come on inside and rest while she finishes preparing dinner."

Entering the small but pleasant home, Jim took a seat and rolled a smoke. While Ralph stuffed an old corn cob pipe with tobacco, Jim looked over and saw Marge and Cindy chatting like old friends. After Ralph had lit his pipe, he asked, "What was that surprised look you gave us when we rode in, Ralph?" Hearing the question, Cindy paused and looked over at the table.

Ralph exhaled slowly. "Didn't mean to offend you, Jim, but the only place this road leads to is Deer Creek Valley. Are you aware of all the killings that have taken

101

place over there this spring and summer?"

"In Helena there was some talk of it, but I didn't pay much attention to it," he replied cautiously. "Marge and I were thinking of investing in the Johansen Mine Works and purchasing a small ranch. We figured any trouble would have blown over by the time we got out there."

"Well, from what the people leaving the valley tell us it sure hasn't blown over yet!" Ralph continued, "Every few days a wagon comes through here with people heading for a new place to live."

"Nobody knows who's behind the killings?" Marge asked.

Shaking the flour off her apron, Cindy spoke up. "There's lots of rumors and speculation, but that's about it. Whoever is doing the shooting is doing it from so far away that no one has even seen the killer."

Jim lit another smoke and pondered the information. None of it made sense. Why shoot all these people? Maybe someone was trying to take over the valley, and this could be a violent way of accomplishing the goal of getting rid of people? Every time someone got killed, several more people moved out. Whatever the motive was, the strategy was working. However, without being able to see the valley and scout around, he might as well save his thoughts on the subject. As Cindy began lighting lamps, the smell of food reminded him how hungry he was.

The door opened and Terry came in, stomping his feet on the rug, "I brushed both of your horses, Mister. I also checked their shoes and other than a small stone in one hoof, everything looks okay."

Thanking him, Jim introduced himself and Marge. Terry nodded and went to wash up for dinner. When they were all seated at the table, Cindy said grace, and then everyone helped themselves. The steaks didn't taste like beef and Jim commented on it.

"You're right," Ralph said. "I was up in the foothills hunting a couple days ago. Those are Elk steaks."

"Well they certainly are tender and have a wonderful flavor," Marge commented.

After dinner, while the women cleaned up, the men went out on the front porch. Jim rolled a smoke and admired the evening sky where the first of the stars were just beginning to appear. "There's nothing like a day's ride and a good meal to relax a person."

"You got that right," Ralph agreed. "So, did you two decide to sleep in the barn or under the lean-to behind the house?"

Jim smiled, "I think we'll just take our bedrolls out back. It'll be quieter and smell a whole lot better than the barn."

After Ralph had finished smoking his pipe, he said goodnight and went inside. A few minutes later Marge came out and put her hand on Jim's arm. Giggling, she teased him, "So, Mister McClair, did you bring enough blankets to keep us warm?"

Surprised at her boldness, he kept a straight face, "I thought you would be warmer in the barn while I slept outside."

Seeing the twinkle in his eyes, she lightly punched him on the arm, "Let's get moving, before I do make you sleep outside by yourself!"

* * *

Shortly after daybreak the sound of chopping wood woke them. Giving Marge a gentle kiss, Jim said he'd go saddle the horses and get ready to head out. "We've got to put a lot of miles under out belts today."

Not wanting to get up, but realizing he was right, she offered to go in and see if Cindy wanted some help throwing a breakfast together.

In the house, Cindy didn't need any help with breakfast, but asked Marge if she would get some clean water for washing up.

As Marge stepped out on the porch and threw the old water on the ground, half a dozen men came galloping up on their horses.

Pausing to study the men, she realized these were not honest cowboys heading down the trail. They all had the dirty and unkempt appearance of men living on the edge of civilization.

As the men halted their horses, one of them noticed her standing there. "Look what we got here, boys! Ain't she the prettiest little thing we've seen in weeks?"

Another chimed in, "How about we show her some good old western charm?" Amid a chorus of agreement and crude comments, the men began dismounting.

Recognizing the dangerous situation that was developing, Marge stepped back inside. "Cindy? Where are you?"

"I'm right here," Cindy said, as she came out of a back room. "I heard horses coming and went down in the root cellar to bring up some more food for the travelers."

"Well, they may be travelers, but they're not looking

104

for breakfast. Where are Ralph and Terry?"

Cindy was starting to get scared by the way Marge was acting. "They split the last of the firewood this morning, so Ralph hitched up the wagon and took Terry along to get a fresh supply. Why? What's wrong?"

"There isn't any time for explanations right now. Do you have a shotgun?" Cindy nodded her head nervously. "Grab it, check the loads, and stay by the back door in case anyone tries coming through there."

Picking up her rifle, Marge stepped back out onto the porch. Wondering where Jim was, she pointed the rifle at the ground in front of the men. "You boys get back on those horses and continue down the road. There's no food here...or anything else for that matter."

Surprised to see a woman casually holding a gun on them, the men paused. Finally, a lean man with a scar across his face spoke up. "These are my boys, lady. We've been riding hard the last couple of days and we need food and rest for the horses. I suggest you put that rifle away and nobody will have to get hurt...real bad anyway," he leered.

While the leader was speaking, one of the men at the edge of the group began to gradually side step to the end of the porch. Watching the movement out of the corner of her eye, and listening to the ugly tone in the man's voice, Marge knew she needed to alert Jim and slow down the threat. Swinging her rifle, she shot from the hip. The slug caught the man by the porch in the leg and he fell over screaming.

"The bitch shot me," he started yelling. "There's blood pumping all over the place...she must have hit an artery."

Nobody was listening to the dying man, however,

105

because as soon as Marge fired her rifle, the men scattered and took positions anyplace they could find cover. Meanwhile, Marge had quickly stepped behind one of the support posts on the porch.

The leader yelled out from behind the water trough, "You're going to die real hard and slow for what you did to Tony. Your own mother won't recognize you when we get done."

Hearing the continuing exchange of words over by the house, Jim had walked to the stable doors just in time to see Marge swing her rifle up and fire. Grabbing the .45 from his holster, he was raising it to take aim at one of the men when he suddenly felt the barrel of a gun shoved against his back.

"Hold it right there, Mister," said a low, deadly voice. "Drop that gun and get your hands in the air. Hey, Boss! I've got the drop on a man out here in the stable. It looks like we got us a hostage."

Hearing this, the leader got an evil grin on his face. "Did you hear that lady? That must be your old man Joey's got covered. Now, we're going to stand up and you'd better not fire, or Joey's gonna blow his brains all over the ground."

Motioning to his men, they all stood up and began to walk towards the porch. At the same time, Joey followed Jim out into the yard. The end of the barrel was pressed against the back of Jim's head and left no doubt what would happen if the trigger was squeezed.

Damn! The leader must have sent one of his men in the back way as an ace up their sleeve, Marge thought. Well, they had Jim as a hostage and there was nothing she could do as the men walked cautiously closer.

When they got about twenty feet from her and had no

where to hide, she quickly swung the rifle to her shoulder and aimed at the leader's chest. Once again, the men stopped their advance. With a determined look on her face, she said, "It looks like we have a standoff."

The leader could not believe this was happening. "Lady, don't you know we'll kill your man if you don't put your rifle down?"

Marge had wondered why Jim would talk about the general stupidity of people. Now she could understand his comments. She calmly asked the leader, "Are you really that much of a moron? Don't you know what a standoff is? You kill him and you're getting the first bullet." Speaking loud enough for everyone to hear, she added, "And I'll shoot at least two others before the rest get to safety."

"She's bluffing!" yelled a man.

"Yeah," another one shouted, "besides, she's only one woman."

"You're not the one looking down the barrel of a rifle, so just shut up Seth," the leader yelled. "Listen lady, what's it going to take for you to stop pointing that rifle at my chest?"

"First, Joey's going to take his gun away from Jim's head and since Jim could still get hit in a cross fire, I obviously won't start shooting. Then all of you worthless scum are going to get on your horses and ride out of here."

What about Tony?" one of the men asked. "He looks dead and needs to be buried."

"I forgot all about him," Marge shrugged. "Two of you men walk over and get his body. Keep your guns holstered! Since he was your friend...you bury him."

As the men mounted their horses and began to slowly

head down the road, the leader yelled back, "We'll run into each other again, lady. When we do, you're going to be sorry you didn't just let us have our way to begin with."

The sound of her rifle fired in the air ended that monologue, and sent the men galloping down the road.

Jim rushed back to the stable, got his gun and ran back out to Marge. As Cindy came out of the door holding the shotgun and looking pale, he grabbed Marge and gave her a big hug. "I'm so glad your okay. You don't know how grateful I am you didn't give up your rifle. I can only imagine how many people have died after giving up their bargaining position in a standoff."

"Oh, Jim," she sobbed, "I was so worried you would get killed."

"We're okay now," he assured her. "Did you notice those men headed in the direction of Deer Creek Valley?"

"No, I was so shook up that I wasn't paying attention to which direction they rode. I wonder why men like that are going there."

Just then, Ralph came pulling into the yard. Bringing the team to a halt, he jumped down and asked what the shots were all about. Marge explained what had happened and assured him no one was hurt.

Running over to Cindy, Ralph gently took the shotgun out of her hands and put his arm around her protectively. "We were farther up the canyon, collecting firewood, when we heard a shot," he explained. "By the time we got the horses hitched back up, there was another shot. We got here as fast as we could. I'm sorry Terry and I weren't here. They might not have tried something if more people had been around."

"Don't feel bad," Jim said. "More people around might have started an actual gun battle. As it was, a fight was avoided because Marge was able to get them into a standoff." Chuckling, he explained how she had made them back down.

"Gosh," Terry exclaimed, "I would love to have seen that!"

Ralph told Terry to stop dreaming of gunfights and go take care of the horses. After he left, Ralph asked what they were going to do.

Jim explained they would still get their horses ready to ride, but would wait a couple hours before leaving. This would give the outlaws time to get far enough ahead, so they wouldn't have to worry about running into them on the road again.

"Well, hang around here as long as you like," Cindy said. "Those men are bad and now they have a score to settle."

Jim assured her they would be careful. While he had several smokes with Ralph, Marge went inside and visited with Cindy. After what seemed like a long enough time, he called her and they mounted their horses. Marge and Jim said goodbye to the family and then turned their horses toward Deer Creek Valley.

Riding down the road, Jim kept a wary eye out for any signs of the outlaws. Whenever they reached a rise in the road, he would take his field glasses and survey the countryside. His cautious attitude finally paid off at one of the hills. He could see the gang had gone down by the river to rest. Studying them, he counted six men and a blanket wrapped body lying by some shrubs.

Turning to Marge, he explained what his plan was. "They're all accounted for, so rather than risk a fight we're going to cut over into that tree line on the far side of the road. If we go slow, and stay quiet, I think we can bypass the gang without them spotting us. Are you ready?" Nodding her head, they skirted the low hill and disappeared into the trees.

After traveling like this for a couple of miles, he felt they were safe and headed back to the road. Once there, he told her they needed to make some good time, because they could not give the outlaws a chance to accidentally catch up to them.

"That sounds good to me! The horses are rested, and I'm on edge knowing their behind us, so let's get riding." Kneeing their horses into a ground eating trot, they soon put several more miles between them and the gang.

Finding a secluded spot for the night, Jim ground hitched their horses and settled down to roll a smoke. "We can't build a fire tonight, because we have no way of knowing where they might be, and we don't want to risk anyone seeing the fire, or smelling the smoke from it.

For a cold supper though, I have some jerked beef in my saddle bag and a can of peaches." Finding the fruit, he opened it with his knife and handed it to her.

Gratefully accepting something besides dry beef, she ate most of the can. "You know, Jim, under different circumstances I could make a comment about the sticky syrup."

Laughing, he told her to get some rest while he stayed up to keep watch. After Marge went to sleep, Jim walked away from the horses and kept a vigil through the night. Towards morning, he jerked with a start and realized he had fallen asleep. Hurrying back to camp, he was relieved to see everything was okay. Waking Marge, he told her the sun would be coming up pretty soon. "Since we can't make coffee, we might as well just get started."

Marge got up and shook her long beautiful hair. She noticed Jim staring at her. "Are you just going to gawk at me like a teenage boy, or get the horses cinched up?"

Flustered, he got the horses ready, and they rode off as dawn approached.

After about an hour on the road, Jim took out his field glasses and studied the road behind them. Seeing no sign of movement there, he turned the glasses to the land in front of them.

In the distance he could see a farm, and farther on he could make out a cluster of buildings. "We must be on the edge of the Valley," he said. "The town of Deer Creek looks like its only two or three miles away, but distances are deceiving out here. It's probably more like ten miles ahead of us."

"Well, I can't wait to get there," Marge said. "I enjoy your company, but not knowing how far back those men are, gives me the creeps."

Nodding in agreement, they settled back into a trot

111

and soon came close to the first farm Jim had seen. Slowing their horses down as they passed the farm, she observed, "The place looks abandoned. This time of morning, everyone should be outside working."

He somberly agreed with her as they continued their journey. Several times they lost sight of the town as the road dipped and looped around hills, but soon they were within half a mile or so.

Slowing their horses to a walk as they approached the edge of town, he noticed some of the buildings appeared deserted. Curious, they rode into town and soon saw people moving around. Several of them stopped to stare as they rode past, but nobody said anything. When they got to the center of town where there were a couple of saloons and a general store, Jim stopped and asked a man sweeping the boardwalk where they could find the Johansen Mine Works.

Eyeing Jim suspiciously, the man answered, "Keep going through town. When you come to the telegraph office, turn right. The main office is three or four blocks down."

Thanking the man, he turned to Marge and shrugged his shoulders at the man's attitude. Continuing down the street, they passed a Land Title company and then came to the Telegraph office.

Marge noticed the place was open, and told Jim to wait for a minute while she ran in and wired the governor. "I want to let Wilson know we've arrived. I'm also going to send a brief wire to Callie"

Several minutes later, she came out with a puzzled look on her face. After she mounted her horse and they had turned toward the mining office, he asked what had happened in the telegraph office.

"I'm not sure," she answered with a frown on her face. "Working for the Pinkerton Agency, I learned how to work with Morse code. When I sent the telegram to Wilson, the operator sent it to Mr. Hartman. You remember him, don't you?"

Jim thought for a moment, "Yeah, I remember him. I thought he had beady little eyes and the face of a weasel."

Laughing at the image, she continued, "Anyway, since Hartman is Wilson's assistant, I didn't think too much of it. However, when I sent a telegram to Callie and informed her of our arrival, and that we would start investigating tomorrow, the operator also addressed it to Hartman. Since it was unusual, I didn't let on that I knew what he had done."

Contemplating what she had told him, Jim commented, "I don't like the sound of it. Whoever is running this theft and murder ring must have the operator paid off so that all information going to Helena is sent to Hartman. It probably explains why Wilson hasn't been able to help do anything about the situation out here. Hartman conceals, or changes any messages received, and when Wilson sends a telegram Hartman modifies the outgoing message as well. It's really a pretty clever operation, actually."

Considering what he said, she added, "The person behind all this must be very meticulous to have paid so much attention to details like these."

"You know what this means, don't you Marge?"

"I sure do. Hartman didn't know who we were, or where we had gone to. But now when he reads those telegrams, he'll know what we're up to and send a message back here. Once the person in charge finds out about

113

us, it's going to become dangerous."

"We're going to have to be very careful," Jim agreed.

After reaching the mining headquarters, they surveyed the area and dismounted. The building looked well constructed, with a heavy stone foundation. There were a few newer buildings around, but most were older, like the mine office. Watching men walking down from the hill, where the sound of heavy extraction equipment was coming from, he observed the mining operation was quite large.

As Marge stepped up onto the porch, she turned back to Jim. "Are you coming in?"

"I'm right behind you," he replied, following her into the front office. On the walls were old black and white photographs of mining operations from earlier days. Along one wall, there was a display of basic tools used by the miners. Prominent in the display was a glass covered case with a pile of small gold nuggets. Towards the back wall were several filing cabinets and a large roll top desk. Sitting at it was a small, old man, with spectacles slid down on his nose.

When the man had finished entering some numbers in a ledger, he looked up. "Hello there, folks. My name is Sam Winchell. I'm in charge of the books for equipment and supplies. Can I help you with something?"

They both said hello, and then Jim continued. "I'm Jim McClair and this is Marge Cl...," feeling a nudge from her, he quickly added, "This is my wife, Marge. We'd like to speak with Brad or Jason Johansen."

"Well," Sam paused, scratching his beard. "Brad's up at the refining plant and Jason is overseeing new timbers being placed in "shaft #7". But it's almost lunch time so one of them should be coming back shortly. You could

114

wait here, or go down to one of the saloons and come back later."

"What would you like to do," Jim asked Marge.

"After missing breakfast, some lunch sounds good." Turning back to Sam, she told him, "We'll come back in an hour or so. Would you please let Brad, or Jason, know we're looking for them?"

"Yes, Ma'am," Sam replied. "By the way, don't go into the Red Dog Saloon. That's where all the miners go to relax, and taking a pretty woman in there will bring you nothing but trouble."

Thanking him for the tip, they left and walked their horses back downtown. Seeing all the men going into the Red Dog Saloon, and some staggering out, he knew that wasn't the place to go...woman or no woman. On the opposite side of the street, and down a couple of buildings, they found a much smaller saloon that looked pretty tame.

Hitching the horses to a rail, they entered the quiet bar. Other than three old timers sitting at a far table, the place was empty. Jim found a table by a window where he could keep an eye on their horses, and motioned the barkeep over.

Wiping his hands on a towel, the barkeep came over and asked what they wanted.

"The sign says you have fresh stew, Jim commented, as he studied the man. "What does fresh mean to you?"

"My wife just made it yesterday, Mister."

Jim smiled, "That's fresh enough for us. How about two bowls of stew and any bread you might have. Could you also bring me a beer?"

"It's been a long ride," Marge spoke up. "Bring me a beer, too."

When the food and drink arrived, they ate in comfortable silence. After the bowls were taken away, Jim got out the fixings for a smoke. While talking and sipping their beers, he noticed a young man walking toward the horses. Leaning forward to see better, he saw the man was looking at the long wooden case strapped to the back of Whisper.

Realizing Jim was no longer listening, Marge turned to see what had gotten his attention. The sight of a man lingering by their horses and nervously looking around made her angry. "I suppose you had better go chase him off. Since he's ruined this moment, hit him once for me if he makes any trouble."

Grinning at her command, he stood up and adjusted his holster. Removing the thong off the hammer, Jim stepped out on the boardwalk and asked him what he was doing.

Startled, the man looked up. "I was just admiring this piece of woodwork." Regaining his composure, he added, "Why don't you go back inside and mind your own business."

"That happens to be my horse, boy," Jim said, as he stepped off the boardwalk. "So that makes it my business."

. The man was young and too inexperienced to recognize the coldness in Jim's eyes, and foolishly snapped back, "I ain't your boy, Mister." When Jim didn't answer, he became bolder, "Maybe I like your case so much that I'll just take it as a souvenir."

This young buck might live to grow up, Jim thought. But, whether he did or not, he was going to learn a lesson in respect. Suddenly, with no warning, Jim backhanded the punk across the side of his face.

116

As the man reeled from the blow, Jim stepped in close and grabbed him by the shirt. Before he could recover, Jim smiled and said, "Marge asked me to deliver this to you." Letting go of the shirt, he hit the man as hard as possible on the jaw. The sharp crack of knuckles against bone was the last sound the troublemaker heard before he lost consciousness and fell limply to the ground.

* * *

Leaving the unconscious man lying in the street, they rode back to the mine office. Hitching their horses next to a large mustang tied to the rails, they went inside. Standing by the desk, in a dusty suit, was a distinguished looking gentleman. From his bearing, Jim could tell this must be one of the owners.

The man stepped forward. Reaching his hand out for Jim to shake, he introduced himself, "Hi, my name is Brad Johansen. You must be Jim McClair and I presume this is your lovely wife, Marge? I understand you were looking for me or my brother."

Jim explained they were interested in the mine and maybe purchasing a small ranch in the area.

Brad shook his head, "We've got all the owners, and headaches we need right now, and we don't require any more investment money. As far as the ranch goes, there are a lot of them available since someone started shooting people this spring. However, I doubt if you'll be able to buy one of them, because as soon as they come up for sale, the Big Sky Company buys 'em out."

Marge interrupted, "I think we have a proposition you'll find interesting. Maybe we could have a private conversation...perhaps over a drink?"

Curious as to what this big man and beautiful woman had in mind, Brad agreed. "I've been up since midnight and finally got a problem straightened out at the smelter, so I'm taking the rest of the day off. You're welcome to come with me to our place, and after I get cleaned up we can talk. I don't know what good it will do, but I'll at least give a man, or woman," he smiled at Marge, "a chance to explain themselves. Follow me," Brad said, as he put his hat on. Before he reached the door, he turned to Sam, "Would you tell Jason I have company at the house and to come there as soon as he gets in?"

"Sure thing boss," Sam replied, as he went back to working in his ledger.

Swinging up on his horse, Brad saw the two wooden cases on Jim's horse. "I don't know what's in the large case, but the small one looks like it holds those fancy telescopes surveyors use. We don't have any use for surveying land out here, if that's what you're thinking of."

Jim chuckled, "You have a good eye, but the last thing I would use it for is surveying."

Not understanding what sounded like a joke, Brad shook his head, "Whatever. Let's get back to the house. You two can rest while I get cleaned up."

Arriving at the big, two story house, Marge was impressed. The yard was very tidy and there were flowers growing in pots on the porch. Commenting on it, she asked about them.

"Oh, that's nothing. The woman who takes care of the house for us insists flowers give the place a warm and friendly atmosphere. She does the work, and since it brings her happiness, we told her to have at it."

Entering the house, Brad led them into a parlor. Soft comfortable chairs were spaced around the opening to a huge fireplace. Other than the chairs, the place had the definite feel of men. Hanging from the walls were numerous deer and elk antlers. Along one wall there was even the head of a grizzly.

Brad noticed what Jim was looking at and told about the time, a few years ago, when he and his brothers had been hunting and came across this grizzly. Describing the hunt, he became quite animated and Jim could tell he enjoyed getting up in the mountains.

Finishing the story, Brad walked over to a bar. Opening it, he pointed at the selection, "Help yourself to anything in here. I'll be back in a little while."

Pouring two light whiskeys, Jim carried them back to the sofa and handed one to Marge.

Taking a small sip she looked around, "I didn't know a person could live so well this far out in the wilderness."

"Yes, this is very impressive. Have you ever thought about living out here in the west?" he asked.

She considered, "This wide open country does grow on a person. I think I could live in this territory, but what would a person do for a living? I'm a hard worker, but I have no desire to work from sun-up to sun-down and burn myself out by the time I'm forty."

"I feel the same way," Jim laughed, "but I'm already past forty, so I guess I'll try not to burn myself out by fifty." He was just beginning to explain how he received money from investments when they were interrupted by Brad walking through the parlor door.

"Sorry for keeping you two waiting so long," he said, while walking over to make himself a drink. After settling down in his own chair, he asked. "So what's this proposition you have for me?"

Marge spoke first, "That was simply a tactic to get you alone. We didn't want anyone to know who we really are, though I'm afraid our cover is already blown and we haven't even been in town a day."

Making a motion with his hand to stop, Brad said, "Back up. What are you talking about? Maybe I should ask who you are first?"

"Sorry, I guess that did sound kind of confusing."

Marge went on to explain who they were and that Wilson had sent for her to try and find out where the missing gold had gone. Just as important, Wilson wanted to know who was behind the theft and if there was any connection between that and the killings in the valley.

Jim interrupted, "The unsolved killings are why Wilson sent for me. I have experience with snipers and he hoped that I could locate the shooter and stop him."

Brad nodded, "that explains the surveyor's telescope. You needed something to let you see farther than the scopes used on some of those fancy rifles."

Turning back to Marge, Brad asked what she meant by "having their cover blown."

Explaining what had happened at the telegraph office, she voiced her suspicions about the governor's assistant, Mr. Hartman. "If we're right about the missing gold and shootings being related, then we could all be in danger once the person in charge is informed about us."

Brad nodded, "You're right about being in danger! As for myself, I believe two big events like this have to be related. For the life of me though, I can't figure out what the motive could be. Oh sure, getting free gold by stealing it from mining companies or prospectors is an obvious motive, but why the killings?"

As Jim began to question him about the shooter, the front door slammed and in walked another man. Waving him over, Brad introduced Jason. After introductions were made, Brad went on, "He's the youngest of us three brothers. We had been looking for a break out west to make our fortune and we really didn't want to spend thirty hard years building up a cattle ranch, so we looked at mining. Then Jason had an idea..."

Everyone paused as Jason laughed and went over to

grab a beer. Opening it, he said, "I'd like to tell my own part in the story, Brad, if you don't mind?"

Having a sip of his drink and taking out the makings for a smoke, Jim asked, "So what was the idea, Jason?"

"Well, we knew that wandering the mountains looking for some elusive "mother lode" was going to be way too difficult, and the odds were stacked against us. Also, the cost of opening up a new mine from scratch is very expensive. So my idea was to look at abandoned mines, or mining towns."

"What would be the point?" Marge asked. "Surely, the mines, or towns, had been abandoned because they were played out?"

Emptying a third of the bottle in one long swallow, Jason continued. "You would think so, and that's what most people would say. However, after looking at several locations, I realized there was still quite a bit of gold to be mined. The problem was the technology to extract it wasn't available. So, while Brad and Mike…," Jason turned to Brad, "When is Mike supposed to be in?"

Looking at the grandfather clock standing against the wall, Brad shrugged. "He should be back in about an hour. But I'm sure after making the freight run, he'll swing by the saloon before coming home."

Jason apologized, "Sorry about losing my train of thought. Where was I? Oh, that's right. I was explaining what we did. Anyway, about ten years ago, Brad and Mike started scouting the western territories. While they searched for and made a list of abandoned mines, I went back east and spent two years at a Mining and Engineering school.

At the school I learned about new extraction methods that would allow a company to go back in and open up

122

old mines. While traveling through this territory, Brad met John Wilson and they hit it off. When I returned, we now had the knowledge to make these old mines profitable, but no money to get the business started."

Brad interrupted, "It's my turn. I went back to Wilson and told him of our plans, and that we would supply everything else for the operation if he knew of someone who could finance it. After checking out Jason's claim of new technology, Wilson decided he would be our investor.

The mine has been a steady producer and everything was going along just great, until last year when we lost over three hundred pounds of gold. And this spring, when we went to make another shipment, several hundred more pounds of gold was missing. Then the shootings started up this year. Now our sweet little operation, and this valley, is going to hell in a hand basket." Sighing, he went to make another drink.

Jim turned to Marge, "We both have a lot of questions to ask, but why don't you go first. I'd like to wait until Mike gets here, since he's more familiar with the coming and goings of people and shipments."

After Brad returned, Marge said, "Wilson gave us a general outline of what happened with the gold. Apparently, there was some switch that occurred?"

"Damn right there was a switch! Last year we didn't find out until the railroad agents checked our bill of lading. This year, we checked our own inventory before shipping and discovered the theft."

Jim smiled, "Wilson did say you were fit to be tied."

Brad grinned ruefully, "Yeah, my brothers thought I was going to have a stroke on the spot. Anyway, after we put a guard down in the basement, no more gold disappeared. However, what we lost is over three hundred thousand dollars and we want it back! But, since we can't even figure out how the switch occurred, then how do we find out who's behind it?"

Marge turned to Jason, "I understand the gold is kept in a locked basement of the mine headquarters. Before you put a guard on it, was there any way for a person to enter?"

"We've always had a guard. We just never had one in the basement before. I'll show you tomorrow, but there are no windows down there and the walls are solid stone. Furthermore, there is only one stairs leading down and it has a heavy steel door at the top. Brad, Mike and I are the only ones with access to the keys, and one of us unlocks the door when anyone needs to enter."

"There's got to be an explanation," Marge said.

"We know there is," Brad blurted out with frustration, "but what?"

As she was about to ask more questions, they heard horses galloping up. Stepping over to the window, Brad announced Mike's arrival.

Laughing and shouting, Mike and two others hitched their horses and walked up the steps. Flinging the door open, the first man through yelled, "Who the hell do those horses belong to?" Seeing a woman sitting in one of the chairs, he paused, "Sorry for cursing Ma'am. I'm not used to coming home in the evening and finding a lady around, certainly not a beautiful one."

Marge flushed at the compliment, "that's okay, I've heard much worse over the years."

Annoyed at the interruption, Jason introduced everyone. "This is Mike. He's responsible for all freight and gold shipments. Please excuse him, Marge. He has a blunt way of talking. The man standing to his right is Justin. He rides as a scout for the wagon and watches out for ambushes. The one on the left is David. He's the lead foreman in charge of getting the crude ore out of the mines and to the smelter."

Marge studied them. Mike was a tall, lean, and hard looking man. She could imagine he would not take kindly to anyone trying to rob him on the road. Justin had an intense, penetrating look in his eyes and she figured he was equally good at making sure the wagons had advance notice of any problems. David had the confident look of someone used to getting hard work done under harsh conditions. All in all, the group appeared to be a good match for each other. She also noticed that while Mike and Justin carried six guns on their hip, David carried a sawed off shotgun in a modified holster.

"That's an unusual weapon for a man to carry out here," she stated.

David stepped forward and nodded at her. "You see Ma'am, a lot of the work I do is down in the mines. When I come up out of the shafts, the bright sunshine hurts my eyes. So if something happens, I need to be able to react quickly without worrying how accurate my fire is. All I need to know with this baby," as he patted the side of the barrel, "is what direction trouble is coming from.

Jim laughed, "I'll bet it stops a lot of problems real fast."

David just grinned as he went over to get himself a beer.

While they relaxed, Brad and Jason brought the other three up to speed on Marge and Jim, and why they were here.

Lighting a cigar, Mike exhaled a cloud of blue smoke and asked, "So what's the plan then?"

Jason explained that he would take Marge over to the mining office first thing in the morning to have a fresh look at everything, while Jim had waited until Mike arrived before asking questions about the shootings.

"Well, I can tell you it's a real bitch out there," Justin spoke up. "People have been trying to come in from the farms or ranches before first light and then staying in town until dusk. But old man Henderson made a mistake and was shot two days ago."

"Why are people taking those precautions?" Jim asked.

Taking over, Mike explained, "Whoever is doing the shooting, only kills during the day. So people figure if they travel before sunrise, or after dark, then it will be safer. Unfortunately, someone will be careless, and get caught in between town and their home while there is still enough light to sight in a rifle."

"That makes sense," Jim commented. "The sniper is working from long distances and is unwilling to come in closer, so he only works during daylight hours."

"Hasn't anyone been able to track this man?" Marge asked.

"No, we've tried," Brad said, with evident disgust. "We've sent an entire vigilante posse out several times to try and find tracks. The shooter is definitely a professional, because he only fires one shot...even if he misses, which has happened a few times over the summer.

Usually, hours have passed by the time we find the victim, and then we have to try figuring out what direction the shot "probably came from". To make matters

126

worse, we have no idea if the shooter is firing from 200 yards or half a mile. And when tracks are found, we don't know if they're made by the shooter or someone else just riding around."

Before anyone could continue, Jim spoke up, "I have more questions, but it's getting late and I need to take care of our horses. Let's continue this later, okay?"

"Justin and I can take the horses out to the stable and get them bedded down," David offered.

Jim thanked him, and said he would first come out to get a couple things off his horse first.

Jason volunteered to cut up a beef roast and slice some bread. "That is, if you don't mind eating a cold supper tonight?" he asked. Everyone agreed that would be fine.

After Jim came back in with the long wooden case and his saddle bag, Brad showed him and Marge to a spare bedroom they could use while staying in town. "Since you're working with us, you might as well stay here," he pointed out.

When he left, Jim placed the case carefully on a dresser and turned to Marge with a sly grin on his face. "I'm starting to get used to this "husband and wife" treatment we're getting."

She stood there with her arms crossed, and pretended to pout. "Aren't you ever planning on making an honest woman out of me, Mr. McClair?"

He hemmed and hawed for a little while, then laughed, "How about if we sleep on it?"

She teased him, "Maybe...maybe not. Right now, we have to get back downstairs and find out more about this sniper."

Downstairs they found everyone making cold beef

sandwiches. In between bites, Mike told them to help themselves. The meat and bread had already been cut into slices. That, along with a jar of pickles and a wedge of cheese seemed to be dinner.

After Marge and Jim had each made a sandwich, they settled down by the fireplace. A fire had already been started, and even though it was summer the evenings were cool enough to enjoy the warmth of the blaze.

Finishing the food, Mike refreshed their drinks and asked Jim what other questions he had about the sniper.

"I'd like to get an idea of where he's been striking. Do you have a map of the area?"

Jason set his beer down. "Just a minute, I've got one in the study." Bringing the map back and laying it on a table that David had cleared, he asked if there was anything else he could get.

Jim thought for a moment, "Yes, do you have a handful of dried beans?"

Brad snorted. "Dried beans and a map? That's a hell of a way to look for a shooter. What ever happened to tracking?"

Knowing what Jim had in mind, Marge interrupted, "He plans on placing a bean in the area where a body was found to see if there is any pattern to the shootings. Right, Jim?"

"That's right," he replied. He looked over at her with increased respect for the quick grasp of his plans, and thought about how in tune the two of them were with each other. Looking over the map, he asked everyone to start remembering where bodies had been found during the summer.

"Well, we might as well start with old man Henderson," Justin said. "He was killed right about here."

128

Placing a bean on the map, where a small canyon branched off the eastern slope of the valley, he added, "Its been real obvious the shooter never bothers anyone traveling the main road between here and Helena. I don't know what you make of that."

Jim considered the information. "There are probably a couple reasons the road is safe for travel. The first is that somebody probably wants people to leave and won't discourage them by making their exit difficult.

The second, more than likely, is the people involved also have to be able to travel back and forth to Helena." Jim paused, "I'm assuming both the gold theft and the shootings are connected." Looking around at the general nod of agreement, he continued, "then the person running the operation is smart enough to know if some people got shot traveling the main road, and others kept getting through safely, then suspicions would be raised."

Taking a moment to roll a smoke, while the men tried to remember where the bodies had been found, Jim leaned over to Marge, "I think I'm going to head out first thing in the morning, before anyone in town has a chance to keep an eye on me. What about you?"

She spoke softly as the men argued about locations on the map. "Jason said he would show me around the mining headquarters tomorrow morning. Other than that, I'm just going to play it by ear."

Nodding, he turned back to the men hovering over the map.

Brad looked up, "I think we have most of the bodies accounted for. Three or four of the earlier ones are missing, because we can't remember where they were found, but we've all agreed the map is fairly accurate."

At first glance, the beans appeared to be scattered all

over the valley. Looking closer, however, Jim saw there were no beans in the northwestern part of the valley. Pointing this out, he asked, "None of you remember any bodies up in this area?"

Looking at each other for a moment, Brad finally spoke, "No, we can't think of any bodies found up there. It's kind of strange, now that we see everything on a map. That part of the valley belongs to the "Rocking Chair P" ranch. Come to think of it, whenever cowboys from there have been in town, nobody's ever mentioned any of their men being shot at, or killed."

"Then I think that area will be a good place to start looking tomorrow," Jim stated.

"I'll be glad to come along and help scout the area," Justin volunteered, glancing over at Mike for permission.

"I appreciate the offer," Jim replied. "However, it'll be better if I hun...I mean travel alone."

Brad and Jason gave each other a knowing look. "If there's anything we can do, just ask," Jason said.

"I'd like to take this map along tomorrow, but I think that's all I need," Jim replied.

The map was left out just in case anyone thought of something else, then everyone settled down for the rest of the evening and visited. Justin, David and the brothers took turns telling stories about adventures above ground, and below. As the evening wore on and the drinks flowed, the stories started to sound exaggerated, but the kidding seemed to be all in good humor, so Marge and Jim kicked back and enjoyed the evening.

When the grandfather clock chimed eleven, Jim got to his feet and held out his hand for Marge. "I think we'll retire so we can get an early start in the morning."

Saying goodnight to everyone, they headed for their bedroom. Climbing up the curved stairs, they could hear laughter coming from the parlor, and the sound of another bottle being opened. Jim smiled to himself and wondered how late this party would last.

* * *

Waking before the sun was up; Jim rolled over and smelled the sweet scent of Marge's hair. Thinking about her, he wondered what it would be like to settle down. She couldn't have kids and he didn't want any, so that part worked out perfect.

Could he live somewhere and just enjoy the company of a good companion? What would they do to keep active and have fun as the years marched by? Oh well, they had to take care of these problems for Wilson first, and if one, or both of them got killed, then those questions and thoughts would be moot anyway.

Sighing, he quietly got up and dressed. Slipping his gun out of the holster, he opened the loading gate and made sure all six chambers were filled. Bending over, he gave her a light kiss on the cheek. Turning to leave, he didn't see Marge open her eyes and smile at his back.

"You be careful, Mr. McClair. I don't want to have to send a search party out for you."

Surprised she had woken up this early, he turned to her. "Don't worry. The thought of you waiting here will make me very careful. Besides, I think the two of us have a lot of mountains to climb and snakes to kill."

"What a quaint way of saying you want to spend time with me."

He smiled and leaned over to give her a passionate kiss and told her to go back to sleep. Picking up his case, he silently closed the door. Going downstairs, he found the kitchen where Brad and Jason were already up, even though they didn't look too good.

Nursing hot cups of coffee, the two looked up and grunted what sounded like "Good morning". Pointing toward the cupboard, Brad told him to find a cup and join them at the table.

After filling his cup, Jim took a sip and laughed, "A little too much "hair of the dog" last night?"

Brad looked up, as Jason groaned, "Don't even talk about last night. Just the thought of it makes my head hurt all over again. If I didn't have to show Marge around today, I'd probably sleep until noon."

Watching the coffee slowly work its magic on the two men, Jim asked if there was anything to eat for breakfast.

"The housekeeper will show up any time now," Jason answered. "She'll fix something for us."

"Well, I'll go and get my horse ready for traveling while we're waiting," Jim said. "I want to get an early start."

Leaving them to stabilize with the pot of coffee, he went out to the barn and found Whisper. Nickering as he walked up, the horse stamped its foot and nuzzled his mouth into Jim's open hand. "That's a good boy, Whisper. We'll be out of here shortly." Hearing the soft rustle of movement behind him, he whirled with his hand on his gun. Seeing Justin walk up, he relaxed. "You always get up this early?" Jim asked.

"Not really, but with you making enough noise to wake the dead, I figured I might as well."

"I just wanted to get out into the timberline before the sun came up," Jim explained."

"Well, unless you need anything, I'm going up to the house," Justin called over his shoulder, as he headed for the door.

After saddling Whisper, Jim rolled a smoke and stood by the open doors. Blowing a cloud of smoke into the darkness, he looked at the morning star. What a beautiful time of day this is, he thought. Most people are still in bed and even the birds and animals haven't begun their morning routines yet. Finishing his cigarette, he led Whisper up to the house and hitched him to a railing. "I'll be back in a little bit," he said, stroking the side of Whisper's neck.

Going into the kitchen, Jim found that the housekeeper had already scrambled up some eggs, and there was a huge platter of sausages. Along with a plate of warmed up biscuits and a jar of preserves was a fresh pot of coffee. Sitting down, he loaded his plate with food and told the men about his general plan for locating the shooter.

Thanking the cook for breakfast, he turned to the men, "I don't know how long I'll be gone, so I would appreciate it if you could keep an eye on Marge. She's an excellent shot and can take care of herself, but it could get dangerous around here."

"Don't worry," Justin said. "Mike told me last night to skip my regular duties and shadow her around."

"Thanks." Standing up to shake everyone's hand, Jim wished them luck in finding out something about the gold. Picking up the small sack of jerked beef and cold biscuits that had been prepared, he tipped his hat and left the room.

Jason turned to Brad, "Do you think he'll succeed?"

Brad thought for a moment, "I think if anyone can, he will. There's something about him. Did you notice his eyes? Sometimes they're filled with humor and compassion, and other times there is a very cold, appraising look about them."

134

Hearing the distant sounds of people talking downstairs, and the rattle of cooking utensils, Marge was unable to fall back to sleep. Lying there, she worried about Jim out in the valley and canyons. He would be at a disadvantage, because the shooter was familiar with the area and all Jim had was a map.

Thinking about it, she realized he had never really told her anything about his experience in undertaking a task like this. He certainly had the confidence needed for the job, but how good was he really?

Deciding she wouldn't be able to relax and go back to sleep again, she got up and dressed. Knowing there would be a lot of walking today, she put on a pair of jeans and boots. Smiling to herself, she thought how silly it was that men expected women to walk around in a dress and dainty shoes all the time. Hell, if it wasn't for strong women, men would probably still be living in caves. Laughing at the image that conjured up, she slipped a small derringer into a pocket that was sewn into her coat. Grabbing her hat, she headed downstairs.

Entering the kitchen, the men stood and greeted her. She could tell they were surprised to see her dressed like a man, but were too polite to say anything.

Returning their greetings, Marge sat down and fixed a plate of food. As she ate, the men quietly sipped coffee and smoked. Finishing her breakfast, she looked up, "Is it too early to start looking around, Jason?"

"Not really, Mike's already opened the office, and by the time we ride down there it will be light enough to start showing you around," Jason said, as he glanced out the window. The first rays of light were already streaking across the eastern sky and it promised to be another hot day in the valley. "I'll go get your horse ready and then we can head on down," he added.

"Thanks, but I'll go with you and saddle my own horse. If I have to be up this early, I might as well start helping."

Putting out the butt of his smoke in an ashtray, Brad stood up. "I've got to get back to the smelter and check on yesterday's repairs. If you need to talk to me about anything, Marge, have Sam send a runner up. Okay?"

"Thanks, I'll keep that in mind."

As Marge and Jason left the kitchen and began walking across the yard, she commented, "You and your brothers seem to have a good working relationship in this operation."

"Thanks...but we're all head strong and things didn't always run this smooth. Years ago, we would try and work on a project together, but ended up arguing about details. After a while it dawned on us that if we separated out the work, and each managed our own responsibilities, then we were all a lot happier and more productive."

Entering the stable, Jason walked over to where the saddles were kept. "You're sure you don't want help saddling your horse, Marge?"

"I've spent a lot of time riding horses and taking care of them," she answered. "I'll be fine." Picking up her saddle and blanket, she went over and began getting her horse ready to ride. Looking around the stable, she was impressed with how nice everything was.

When the horse was saddled, she led it outside and waited for Jason. In the distance, Marge could see a group of men walking up to the mines. As much as she

136

loved the outdoors, she couldn't imagine spending your work day underground. The sound of Jason closing the stable doors broke her train of thought and she mounted up.

Riding down the hill to the mining office, Jason described the town and the people in it. When Marge commented that most of the people they had seen yester-day seemed suspicious of her and Jim, he explained that with everything going on, he wasn't surprised. "People see strangers come into town and naturally wonder what they're up to."

"Speaking of strangers," Marge said. "We had a run in with a small group of bad men at the way station, and after our confrontation they continued in this direction. Have you seen any rough looking men come into town lately?"

Jason laughed, "Most of the men out here would be described as rough. But, no, I haven't seen new faces around town. Now that you mention it though, Mike's told us that on several of his supply runs, there have been small groups of men heading towards Deer Creek Valley.

Mike and his men are so heavily armed that these groups left the supply wagons alone, but he didn't know where the men were going. We just figured they were passing through, or trying to get work at one of the out-lying ranches. Why? What do you make of it?" Jason asked.

"Nothing yet," Marge answered. "It's just one more piece of the puzzle to fit in somewhere."

Continuing down the road, Jason would stop occasionally and chat with a miner about how things were going. "I've found I can keep better track of the mines

137

and complaints by asking the men directly," he explained. "David will give straight talk about what's going on in the mines. However, some of the foremen think problems reflect on them personally, so a lot of their information is watered down just to make themselves look better."

Approaching the mine headquarters, Marge stopped her horse and studied the building. She hadn't really paid attention yesterday, but the headquarters was actually a pretty big structure.

Looking around at the houses in the distance, she pointed to a huge, three story, and run down house about two hundred yards away. It was set apart from all the smaller homes and the yard was over grown with trees and shrubs. "What did that house used to be?"

"The original mine owner lived there," Jason said. I don't know anything about him, though. We picked this property up from the County Courthouse as an abandoned claim. All we had to do was file the paperwork on it and pay the back taxes. Now this whole operation is ours. We even own the first row of houses on the edge of town."

Bringing her attention back to the office, she suggested they walk around the building before going inside.

Hitching their horses, Jason led her around one side of the building and talked as they slowly walked. He pointed out there were no windows going into the basement, and all of the upper windows on the back, and sides, were nailed shut with boards. "Nobody can figure out how the thieves got inside," he added.

Having walked completely around the building, Marge paused on the steps. "So, tell me again, what kind of security did you have here about the time of the thefts?"

"Well," Jason paused, "Until this year, when we got ready for our spring shipment, and found several hundred more pounds of gold missing, we had a guard locked inside the building. Only Brad, Mike, or I have the key to the big lock, so in the morning one of us would come down and let the guard out. Then whoever opened up would wait until Sam showed up for work. Let's go inside before I continue. It will be easier to explain the next part if you see it at the same time."

Opening the door for her, Jason followed her in and asked Sam if everything was okay.

"Nothing going on yet," Sam replied. "However, there was a lot of speculation down at the Red Dog Saloon last night about Marge and Jim showing up yesterday."

"Sam," Jason smiled, while shaking his head, "You know going in there is just asking for trouble."

"Yup," Sam grinned back, "But it's the only place around where a man can have a drink and look at pretty women at the same time. On payday I might even get lucky," he said, forgetting Marge was in the room. Realizing what he had just said, he apologized, "Pardon me, Ma'am. I'm so used to being around men that I forget my manners."

She enjoyed his discomfort for a moment before letting him off the hook. "That's okay, Sam. Everyone knows why those women are in the saloons." Remembering how Jim made love to her, she got a little flash of jealousy thinking of the women he might have entertained in saloons over the years. Chiding herself for being silly, because she enjoyed the company of men which was no different, she turned back to Jason. "Why

139

don't you show me the rest of the security, and anything else you think might be important for me to know?"

Leaving Sam red faced, with his nose buried in a ledger, Jason took her over to a large door at the end of the room. He explained this heavy door also needed a key that only the brothers had access to. Taking a large key out of his pocket, he unlocked the steel door and swung it open. "Wait here a moment and I'll go get a lantern."

While he was gone, Marge looked down into the pitch black stairwell. As the smell of musty air swirled around her, she wondered how anyone had been able to get down there without attracting attention.

"Here you are," Jason said, as he came back. "I brought a lantern for you, also." After she took it, he stepped in front of her and proceeded down the stairs. The steps were solidly built of planks and supported by large posts. As they neared the basement floor, the light cast weird shadows in all directions.

The first thing Marge noticed was the basement consisted of several rooms. There was an open space to their right, but to the left was a wide hallway with doors on each side. "Is this the original floor arrangement?" she asked.

"Yeah, it is. The person who built this put in individual rooms for different storage purposes. The first room on your left is where we keep the payroll and other expense records. The next one is where we keep old maps of the mine shafts and other information related to the mines."

As they walked down the hall, he opened the first door on the right and showed her a room piled with odds and ends; basically a junk room. The next room was empty and then they came to the last door on the right.

Marge looked at the massive steel door and noticed the walls around this room were made of stone, whereas the other rooms had been finished off with wood walls. "This must be the underground vault you spoke of."

"That's right," Jason confirmed. "This room was designed for safe storage, and all the walls are built of stone." Unlocking the door, he stepped inside.

Following him, Marge held up her lantern and saw heavy timbers supporting a stone slab ceiling and that the floor was also made of stone slabs. Short of having a bank vault, this was an impressive room for storing valuables.

"If you'll come over here, I'll show you our current stockpile of gold bars," Jason said.

Walking over to where he was standing by a stack of wooden boxes, she let out a low whistle. If she remembered correctly, Wilson said each box contained one hundred twenty pounds of gold and there had to be at least two dozen boxes here.

Jason smiled, "that usually is the reaction of anyone who realizes how much gold we can recover from what is supposed to be an abandoned mine."

Then he went on to explain that not only was it difficult getting down here, but the bunkhouse, about a hundred yards east of here, always had at least a dozen miners sleeping there. If a gang tried to force their way in, those men would be over here in minutes, each one of them armed with twelve gauge shotguns loaded with buckshot. "That's why we never worry about an armed attack on our vault," he said with a grin.

"I can see why you feel it's safe to store this much gold in one spot," she replied with a wry smile. "But, that must also be why someone had to figure out a de-

141

vious method of getting at it." Raising her lantern higher in the air, she walked over and studied the foundation walls. "What are all these marks from?"

Jason walked over and looked at what Marge was pointing at. "When we checked the inventory before shipping this spring, we found four boxes had been switched with iron, and one of the things we thought about was a fake wall. All those marks are where we smacked at the wall with sledgehammers. They're solid stone," he assured her.

Marge nodded, and walked slowly along the two foundation walls. Studying them, and moving the lantern back and forth, she noticed the west wall had smooth seams along all four edges. Keeping this observation to herself for the moment, she asked to see the room directly across from this one.

Leading her back into the hallway, Jason opened the door to the room across the hall and stepped inside.

Following him, she could see this room appeared to be storage for odds and ends also. A collection of mining tools, along with a clutter of chairs and an old desk shoved against one wall, were the only things in here. Walking over to the west wall, she held the light up and noticed there were no straight seams along the edges in this room.

"Do you see anything that gives you an idea?" Jason asked.

Marge seemed lost in thought for a moment. Ignoring his question, she asked, "Does this room seem smaller to you?"

Jason held up his lantern and looked around. "No, it's just another room in the basement. You can even see where the east walls, in both rooms, are lined up with each other."

She went back to the vault room for a minute, and then came back to where Jason was waiting for her. "Is there anything we can use for measuring?" she asked.

"Well, I don't have a measuring stick, but I could find a length of rope. Would that do?"

"That'll work just fine."

As he went to locate a rope, she looked around the room and thought about some of the elaborate methods of concealment criminals used back east to escape capture by the police. Wondering what the original owner and builder had been like, she was interrupted by Jason's return.

"Here's a rope, Marge. What do you want me to do with it?"

Telling him to hold one end of the rope against the east wall, she took the other end and walked over to the west one. Stretching the rope tight, she held it up to the wall. Tying a small knot where the rope met the wall, she turned to Jason. "Let's go back into the vault room."

Once there, she had him go over to the east wall again. Walking toward the west wall, she held the knot in one hand. As she approached the wall, the slack was taken up in the rope and she ended up holding the knot short of the wall. Smiling to herself, she told Jason to drop the rope and come over by her.

"The rooms are the same size, aren't they?" he asked.

"No! Actually, this room is over a foot longer than the other one." Not wanting to lose her train of thought, she continued, "I want to go back outside now."

When they were upstairs again, Jason took both lanterns and turned them off. Locking the basement door, he asked her what she wanted to do now, and if she was going to tell him what she was thinking.

"Not yet. I'd like to look at the west side of the building once more."

Saying goodbye to Sam, they went out on the front porch where Justin was smoking a cigarette and whittling on a piece of wood. Pausing with the knife, he asked where they were off to now.

"Marge wants to look around out here again," Jason answered. Nodding, Justin went back to carving whatever it was he was making.

Walking around the outside, Marge paused and studied the foundation. Not seeing anything out of the ordinary, she turned and stared at the old house which was directly west of the foundation. Sure enough, the original owners' mansion was in line with the head-quarters foundation and there were no buildings in between.

Standing there, considering the possibilities, she asked Jason to go get the lanterns again.

"What do we need them out here for?"

"We're going to explore the old mansion. There has to be an explanation for every mystery and I've got a hunch."

Wondering what she had thought of, he went back to the office and got the lanterns. After telling Justin what Marge wanted to do, they headed towards the house.

* * *

Stepping over to the end of the porch, Justin watched them. As they reached the house, he noticed a movement in the overgrown trees between the mansion and another old house near by. Keeping a close eye on the area where he thought he saw someone, Justin eventually spotted a man move from behind a tree and head back behind a row of old buildings.

Debating whether he should stay and keep an eye on Marge or follow the man, Justin chose to follow whoever had been hiding over there. He wanted to find out who the man was and where he was going.

Watching the spaces in between the buildings, he saw the man running past them and heading in the direction of town. Putting his knife back in its sheath, Justin quickly ran over by the miner's bunkhouse and cut through an alley.

Stopping at the end of it, Justin peered around the corner. Moments later, a short, skinny man with a pock marked face ran out between two buildings. Seeing the man up close, Justin recognized him as Jacob. Why the hell has he been skulking around and running all over the place, Justin thought to himself?

Crossing the street, Jacob slowed to a walk and went into the "Land & Title Company" office. A few minutes later, he came back out again and ran over to the Red Dog Saloon.

Staying where he was, Justin kept a watch for Jacob to come back out. As he patiently waited, Justin wondered what the hell the man had gone in to see Mr. Williams at the Land Company for.

When about ten minutes had passed and there was

still no sign of Jacob, he decided he had better get back to shadowing Marge.

*

Meanwhile, back at the mansion, Jason had just forced open the front door. The motion stirred up a cloud of dust, which assaulted their noses. Cobwebs were everywhere, and as he brushed them aside pointed out there was no sign anyone had been in here for a long time. Walking down the hallway with Marge close behind, he asked what she was looking for.

"I'm looking for the entrance to the basement." Moving toward the back of the house, they passed by rooms filled with broken furniture. There was also plenty of evidence small animals had been coming into the house, probably during the winter to get out of the cold. "Look Jason, here's the kitchen!"

Entering the room, a person could imagine what the home must have been like in its prime. The kitchen was as big as most cabins on the frontier, with two separate stoves for cooking, and enough cupboard space to handle a small army.

Walking silently through the room, she found a large pantry. At the end of the pantry was an exterior door and on the left side of the pantry was a large interior door. "This must be the basement entrance," Marge said."

Approaching the door, she noticed there was very little dust in this part of the house. Pausing, she pointed at the floor. "See this, Jason? Through here, there's only a thin layer of dust and no cobwebs."

"I see what you mean. Someone has been in here more recently than the rest of the house. What do you make of it?"

"I'm not sure, but hopefully we'll find out. Why don't you light the lanterns and then we'll check out the basement."

Moments later, Jason handed one to her and stepped forward and opened the door. Peering down into the darkness, he told Marge to watch her step and started down.

When they reached the basement floor, they both held their lights high and looked around. The air had the general smell of dust and decay and Marge shuddered at the thought of all the spiders and other creepy little things living down here.

Composing herself, she lowered the light close to the floor, and pointed out the fairly fresh trail going towards the far end of the basement. "This trail through the dust hasn't been used in a while, but it's obviously been made this year," she commented.

Jason nodded in agreement, and they began following the old trail when they heard what sounded like a door opening upstairs. "Did you hear that?" he asked quietly.

"I sure did. Let's set the lanterns down on these old crates and step back into the shadows." Moving away from the light, she slipped her hand into the pocket where her derringer lay. After a few moments, they heard someone yell down into the basement, asking if anyone was down there. She silently shook her head at Jason and the two of them remained quiet.

They could make out the sound of two men arguing about seeing a light, and finally heard soft footsteps on the stairs.

Marge leaned over and whispered to Jason, "Move farther back in the shadows, and when they get down here I'll pretend I'm by myself. But have your gun handy in case something happens." Nodding, he slipped his gun out of the holster and stepped back.

When the two men got to the bottom of the stairs, they moved a few feet apart and looked around. Marge could see they had their guns drawn and appeared confused that no one seemed to be down there.

One of the men finally said in a loud nervous voice, "We know someone is down here, and if you come out, no one will get hurt. Our job is to just run anybody off the property."

Jason almost yelled out that the house was on mining property and he was one of the owners, but luckily kept his mouth shut.

When there was still no response, the other man winked at his partner. "What Fred said is true. We ain't going to hurt no one. You come on out here and we'll all just go upstairs and leave. Okay?"

Realizing the men were staying until they had found someone, Marge motioned to Jason for silence and then called out, "Don't shoot. I didn't answer before because I was afraid, but I'm coming out now." Moving back into the light, the men didn't pay any attention to the fact that she had her right hand in her coat pocket.

Seeing a beautiful woman step forward, with no sign of anyone else, the men relaxed. "Hey, look what we got here, Mitch," Fred said with a leer in his voice. "We have us a pretty little woman who's afraid of the dark. Jacob didn't say anything about this, what do you think we should do?"

Barely able to keep from drooling as he caressed Marge's body with his eyes, Mitch smiled wickedly. "Well, I think we should show the pretty little thing

148

there's nothing to be afraid of down here."

Fred cackled, "Except maybe us."

Noticing she didn't seem frightened, Jason bit his lip to keep quiet and waited for her to make the first move.

As Marge stepped forward, she moved slightly to her right. The men didn't know it, but she had just made sure not to be in any line of fire between them and Jason.

Smiling innocently, Marge said softly, "I guess I'll have to trust you boys to do the right thing."

"Oh, it'll be the right thing...at least for us," Mitch laughed, as he elbowed Fred in the ribs.

Knowing what the men had in mind, Marge didn't offend her dignity by pleading with them...she simply squeezed the trigger of her derringer and then jumped farther to the side.

The little gun was no good for any distance shooting, but in these close quarters it was accurate and deadly. The bullet slammed into Fred's chest and before Mitch could react, Jason opened fire and placed a well aimed slug in his forehead.

As the back of Mitch's head exploded, Fred slumped to the floor and stared unbelievingly at the small hole in his chest. "Look what you've done to me, bitch!"

"It was you or me, asshole," Marge said sarcastically. "Now tell me what you meant, when you said Jacob didn't mention anything about finding a woman down here?"

"Can't you see I need a doctor, lady? Besides, I'm not telling you anything," Fred said, as he tried to put on a brave front.

Dimly becoming aware there was a man standing by her, Fred coughed up blood, and asked, "Where the hell did you come from?"

"I've been standing in the shadows listening to your trash talk to Marge. If you weren't already dying from her bullet, I'd put another slug in you to make sure. Now answer her question and maybe we'll give you a decent burial," Jason angrily told him.

Suddenly, a spasm of pain shot through Fred's chest and he screamed in agony. Seeing the cold look in their eyes, he pleaded, "Please! Don't leave me down here. I'll tell you what I can. Jacob came into the saloon and told us that a couple of people were snooping around this old house and we were to kill them. He gave us a hundred dollars and said we had to hurry."

"Is there anything else," Jason asked, as he kicked Fred in the ribs.

Letting out a long scream, he gasped, "Honest Mister, that's all."

Hearing a door slam upstairs, Marge quickly reloaded her derringer and stepped back. Moments later, they could hear Justin shouting for them. Breathing a sigh of relief, she yelled to him they were in the basement.

As Justin ran down the stairs, Marge turned back to Fred. She noticed frothy blood was bubbling out of his mouth and running down the front of his shirt. "Well Fred, I guess you and Mitch did show me there was nothing to be afraid of down here."

While the man died at their feet, Jason snapped at Justin, "I thought you were supposed to be watching our backs, what the hell happened?"

"I'm sorry. I was watching, but I noticed someone spying on the two of you and then he ran off toward town. I figured you two would be safe enough, so I cut back through an alley to see where he went. When I got close enough I saw it was Jacob."

"Who's Jacob?" Marge interrupted. "Fred mentioned him just before he died."

"He's a sleazy little man," Jason explained, "who runs errands for people around town, mostly for Jeff Williams, the man who owns the Land & Title Company."

"That's the place where Jacob went, when he scurried back to town," Justin said excitedly. "Then he left the Title Company and went over to the Red Dog Saloon."

Considering what had almost happened down here, Justin added, "I had been waiting for Jacob to come back out, but then I got nervous about being gone so long and headed back here. These men must have gone out the back of the saloon, so no one would see them coming up here. I was a hundred yards or so from the house when I heard faint shots and came running. I'm awful sorry, Marge."

"That's okay," she assured him. "We're not hurt, and now we know it was probably this "Mr. Williams" who had Jacob send these men to kill us. Come to think about it, we've learned more in the last few hours than I could possibly have hoped for."

She patted Justin on the arm, "Now that you're here, why don't you stay at the bottom of the stairs in case anyone else tries to bother us. Jason and I will go back to exploring the other end of the basement."

151

* * *

Going back to following the faint trail across the floor, Marge came to a door. Opening it and stepping inside, she could see it had once been an office of some kind.

The walls and ceiling were finished off with pine boards and there was an old, ragged looking, mounted elk head hanging on one wall. Along the east wall was a large desk that had been shoved against it. Scattered around the room were several pieces of broken furniture.

Walking over to the desk, Marge looked at the tracks on the floor. "See this?"

Jason came over and looked at where she was pointing. "Yeah, I see it." In this room, with the door closed, there had been little dust to settle back down and the scuff marks of boots could clearly be seen leading up to the edge of the desk. "Whoever put the desk against the wall figured anyone coming down here wouldn't notice. If it hadn't been for you looking for something unusual, we would never have come across this."

Handing his lantern to her, Jason grabbed hold of the end of the desk and dragged it away from the wall. Once the rest of the wall was exposed, he took his light back and the two of them stood staring at the wall. It appeared to be covered with the same pine boards as the rest of the room.

"Why don't you start on the left, Jason, and work your way back to the center here," Marge told him. "I'll start on the right and work toward you."

"What are we looking for?" he asked, walking along the wall.

"Something that seems unusual or out of place," she

152

explained. "It could be anything, a seam that doesn't fit quite right, or a board that's loose." Following the wall, she moved the light up and down, studying the boards. "Are you finding anything over there, Jason?"

"No, the boards are faded and cracking, but I can't see anything out of place."

Marge took another step to her left and held up the light and saw a wooden pedestal. It had been mounted on the wall for holding a lamp. She was about to take another step to her left, when she paused and stepped back to the pedestal. Reaching up, she pulled on the wood. When nothing happened, she called Jason.

Walking over to her, he asked what she had found.

"I don't know, but there's nothing along the wall except this lamp holder. I'll hold the light up while you try and move it, okay?"

Setting his light down, Jason reached up and tried to pull on the pedestal. When nothing happened, he tried twisting it to the right and then to the left. "The lamp holder seems to be nailed down pretty good."

"Let me take a look," Marge said, as she stepped next to him. Holding her light up, she studied the pedestal frame. "See this, Jason, down here at the bottom of the wood support? Notice this nail right here," she pointed, "is bigger and out of place when you compare it to the pattern of nails in the rest of the frame? Let's see what happens when we take it out."

Jason took out his knife and began working the blade behind the wood frame. Once he had pried the wood loose, he took the butt of the knife and hammered the wood back down. When he did this, the head of the nail protruded slightly. Taking a pair of pliers he carried with him for repairs, he struggled to pull the nail out. After a few moments, it finally gave way with a loud screech.

"I'm not sure what that accomplished," Jason said, as he dropped the nail on the floor. "The frame still has other nails in it."

"There has to be a reason someone put that bigger one in. Try and do something with the pedestal now."

Reaching up, Jason grabbed the pedestal again, and to his surprise it started to rotate when he pushed to the left. "Look Marge! Those other nails must have been cut short and nailed in as a fake front." Continuing to rotate the pedestal to the left, they heard a sharp click and an entire section of wall popped open.

With her heart beating fast, she took hold of the edge of the section and pulled outward. The panel swung open to reveal a dark tunnel. With excitement in her voice, she told him to let Justin know what they had found and that they would be exploring the tunnel.

Marge waited for Jason to return and then they stepped into the tunnel. The air was dank, and she suggested they wait a couple of minutes to let some fresh air enter.

While they waited, Jason pointed out the clear trail of boot prints in the damp, dirt floor. "It's obvious men have been through here. Where do you think it leads to?"

Trying to picture the layout of the buildings in her head, she replied, "Unless I made a mistake, this is the east wall of the house and..."

Jason interrupted, "And this wall is directly across from the west wall of the mining headquarters. Damn! I can't believe something this elaborate even exists."

"You have to consider the siege mentality of the first people out here," she explained. "There were hostile Indians and outlaws everywhere. I can imagine the original owner must have wanted to have a safe and secret way of moving back and forth between these two buildings. Think of the strategy you could employ, if men and supplies could suddenly pop up in another building hundreds of feet away."

"That would certainly have taken attackers by surprise," Jason agreed, as he marveled at the thought of defenders moving around under ground. "The air seems to have improved quite a bit. Are you ready, Marge?"

Holding their lights up high, they entered the tunnel. From what they could tell, it ran in a straight line. When Jason estimated they were about halfway to the mining office, Marge spotted a small chamber along the left wall. Inside they found a pile of picks and shovels.

"This must have been set up as a last resort defense position in case both buildings were over run," Marge speculated. "Defenders in here would have a clear field of fire down both directions of the tunnel. And with these tools, digging out a hole to the surface would have been fairly easy if the attackers blew up the entrances."

"I still can't believe a tunnel has been down here all these years without anyone knowing about it," Jason said.

As they continued along the tunnel, Marge pointed out the obvious, "Well, someone knew, or found out this existed, because it's certainly been used."

Peering ahead into the shadows as they walked, they realized the floor was sloping gently down. Soon they came to what appeared to be a dead end. Swinging their lights around, they saw the tunnel turned sharply to the right and also to the left.

"Let's check out the tunnel to the right," Jason suggested.

Cautiously moving forward, Marge suddenly caught

a glint of light reflecting off metal. Holding her light back in the direction she had seen something, she asked Jason to come take a look at what appeared to be railroad rails. "What do you make of this?"

Jason stepped over and looked down at four rails, each about eight inches apart and covered lightly with a coat of grease. Kneeling down to take a closer look, he hit his forehead on something. "Damn it!"

Rubbing his head as he stood up, Jason raised his lantern and saw a heavy steel cable a few feet above the rail lines. What the hell is this, he wondered. "Marge? Would you step to your left a few feet and raise your lantern higher?" Taking a few steps in the opposite direction, he held up his light and could see a large winch. "What's the cable hooked to on your end?"

Marge turned and moved a little farther down the length of the cable. "It's bolted onto a steel plate, and the plate seems to be anchored to the end face of this stone wall. "What would be the point of having a cable anchored to the wall, Jason?"

"Come over here," he called, "And I'll show you something."

Walking toward Jason, she could hear him laughing. Wondering what he thought was funny; she reached him and asked what he had found.

"Do you have any idea what this is," Jason asked. Shaking her head, he went on. "This is a winch, and a very heavy duty one. Lean over, and you can see where someone has poured oil over all the components to keep the steel from rusting, also, if I'm right, to make the machinery run as quiet as possible."

Puzzled, she looked at the cable and winch. "What's it doing down here, though?"

"I'll explain in a moment. It just feels good to finally surprise you for a change. You're clever, and have accomplished so much in only a few hours that I was feeling kind of useless. However, now I can demonstrate some of my knowledge."

"If you don't start explaining yourself, I'm going to kick you in the shins," she said, with a tone of exasperation.

"Okay, okay. There was a guy I knew at the engineering school who was always building things around his house. His name was Pat, and he would invite me over for dinner with his family once a week. While we waited for dinner, he would show me projects he was working on. Anyway, one time Pat showed me a house wall he had built. I asked him what was so special about an ordinary wall..."

Marge interrupted, "Is this going somewhere?"

"I'm just giving you some background, so this will make sense. While I was looking at the wall, and trying to see something that would make it unique, Pat walked over to a closet and went in. A moment later, the entire wall began moving. Shortly, it had retracted into a wall pocket and we could step into his back yard.

When you told me what the cable was attached to on your end, and I saw this large winch, I remembered what he had done with some creative design engineering. The bottom line is that I think we're looking at a winch and cable that is capable of moving a several ton wall!"

Laughing at the look of bewilderment on her face, Jason elaborated, "Take a look at those rails," he said. "Did you notice, besides the four railroad rails, the railroad ties are also only a few inches apart? And if you look between them, you can see they are resting on slabs

157

of stone. Someone designed and built an incredibly solid and apparently level surface for the wall to roll along the rails on."

She shook her head, "Are you telling me a person operating this winch by hand could move several tons of stone?"

"I sure am. Now, let's see if I'm right." Picking up a steel bar propped against the wall, Jason placed one end into a slot at the end of the winch and began to pull on it.

After a moment of exerting some serious pressure on the bar, the winch began to rotate and Marge could feel faint movement coming from the darkness behind them.

Jason continued to reset the bar and rotate the winch until he figured the cable had moved three or four feet. Stopping to take a rest, he suggested they walk back and take a look."

Picking up his lamp, he led Marge down the tunnel. Now they could both see that what had looked like a dead end wall had moved a few feet in the direction of the winch. Speechless, she just stared at the enormity of the concealed wall.

"Look," he said, "Now that the wall is moved, we can see the rails below it, and here's another cable on this end. It must have been designed so another winch could close the wall from the opposite direction. Pretty clever," and he added, "It must have taken a really good stone mason to design a wall that wouldn't fall apart after a few movements."

Marge stepped up to the opening that now existed and raised her lantern. There, sitting in a nice neat stack, were the boxes containing gold bars. "What a sweet plan the thieves had," she said. "I can understand now why they didn't clean this place out all at once."

Laughing, she added, "The mining company did all the work of extracting the gold and refining it, and then conveniently stored the gold in a vault that the crooks had a backdoor to."

"I don't really see the humor in this," he responded with a curt tone.

"Oh, come on Jason. Think of the irony. Here you brothers have been faithfully guarding the gold from outlaws, while at the same time someone who discovered this secret entrance has been helping themselves to gold anytime they wanted some."

"Well, I'm glad the loss of nearly half a ton of gold is amusing you," he said sarcastically. "But now that we know how entry was gained, I'll have David bring some miners down here and disable the winches. Let's go back up now, or would you find it funny to start knocking on the vault door and give Sam a heart attack?"

Marge held up her hand. "We don't want to block this entrance, and we can't let anyone other than a handful of trusted people know we've discovered the tunnel."

"Why not," Jason asked? "If we seal it up, we can protect the remaining gold."

"That's a short term solution," Marge countered. "The two men who came to kill us are now dead. The person who sent them, and I'll assume it was this Mr. Williams; will soon find out his men failed. He'll start getting real nervous, but won't know if we discovered anything...unless we tip our hand.

I think we should close the rock wall and go back to the mansion. When we get there, let's find that nail you dropped on the ground and pound it back into the pedestal. What we need to do is make the room look like we found nothing. Then, you and Justin can take the bodies of those two men out in back of the mansion and have some miners bury them somewhere."

"What good does that do us?" Jason asked.

She considered his question. "Mr. Williams has to have other people involved. If he gets nervous enough, he may try something else. Since we know about this entrance we can keep a discreet eye on the mansion, and spot anyone trying to come back down here. Other than that, let's just play it by ear, okay?"

"I still don't like it," he grumbled, "But we'll do it your way." He then went to the other winch and closed the rock wall. Walking back through the tunnel, he asked some more questions and the two of them ironed out a general strategy.

Stepping back into the basement room, she reminded him to close everything up the way it was found, and she would go talk to Justin.

A short time later, Jason came back to where Marge and Justin were standing by the dead men. "I've left the room looking undisturbed, Marge. Why don't you hold the lanterns while Justin and I carry these bodies upstairs?"

When the dead men had been placed outside, Marge told Justin to find a good location to keep an eye on the place, and cautioned him not do anything if men entered the house. "We want to find out information, not simply stop anyone from stealing more gold," she explained.

Nodding his head in understanding, Justin went off into the woods, while Marge and Jason circled the house and headed back to the mine office.

Entering the office, they found Brad and Sam talking.

Looking up at Marge, Brad asked if they had found anything.

"Not really," she quickly answered before Jason had a chance to reply. "Did the two of you hear any noises while we were gone?"

"I haven't heard anything," Brad answered, "except a while back we both thought we heard what sounded like muffled gunfire, but neither one of us could tell where it came from. Why?"

"I'll explain later," she said, glancing at Jason with a satisfied smile. After telling Jason that she would like him to go home and organize on paper everything they knew, she turned to Brad and asked if he would accompany her to the Land & Title office.

Puzzled by the request, because he had no knowledge of what had happened that morning, Brad hesitated. Seeing Jason give a slight nod of his head, he recovered smoothly and said he would be glad to escort her there.

* * *

After they left the office, Brad went to untie his horse from the hitching rail.

"Let's not take the horses," Marge said. "There are some things I need to explain before we get to the Land office, and walking will give me time to do it."

Taking what looked like a leisurely stroll toward town, she brought him up to date on what had happened and what her plan was. When she got to the part about two men trying to kill her and Jason, Brad nearly lost it.

"I say we just go in and kill Jeff Williams, that son of a bitch," Brad said hotly, as he gripped the handle of his colt .45.

"This is exactly why I needed to talk to you before we got there," she said, attempting to calm him down. "You have to put on an act when we see Mr. Williams and pretend everything is normal."

"Why? We can link him to the men who tried to kill you and Jason, and his attempt to stop you from invest-tigating the old mansion is evidence enough for me that he's involved in the gold theft."

She stopped walking and grabbed his arm. "We need to find out what happened to the gold...not just who may have taken it. Even more important than that though, we need to find out if Mr. Williams knows anything about the shootings."

"How about if I beat the information out of Jeff instead of killing him," he offered.

She smiled to herself. These western men certainly had uncomplicated ways of looking at problems and how to deal with them. "That's a nice gesture, Brad. But we don't know who his contacts are outside of town. We know he's in touch with Wilson's secretary, Mr. Hartman, and the telegraph operator must also be involved. Other than that, we have no idea what the whole scheme is. Think about it, Brad. Why all the killings? What's the motive? There's so much we have to learn before we play our hand."

Grudgingly admitting she had a point; Brad still wanted to know why he couldn't just force the information from Jeff.

"Because, we have to maintain some semblance of a legal investigation," she patiently explained. "Remember, I'm a Pinkerton agent and Jim is a legal representative of the Territorial Governor. We have to make sure and collect enough evidence for a possible court trial, okay?"

When he had finally been convinced of her approach, they continued on to the Land office. Before entering the building, she reminded him one more time to keep his temper in check and follow her lead.

Opening the door, he followed her into the office. Jeff Williams looked up as they entered and pasted a nervous smile on his face. "Hello, Brad. What can I do for you today?"

Brad took a moment to remind himself this was Marge's game plan and forced a smile of his own, "Hi, Jeff." Nodding toward the woman at his side, he continued, "This is Marge McClair. She's staying at our place with her husband, Jim."

Jeff reached out to shake her hand, "Pleased to meet you, Marge. What brings you and your husband to this out of the way place?"

Marge smiled, knowing that Jeff knew who she was. "Jim and I are interested in buying a small ranch or farm

163

in the area, so Brad brought me over here to meet you. Are there any places available right now?"

"Well, I don't know if you've been told about a crazed killer loose in the valley. But consequently, homes and land have been up for sale all summer long, because farmers and small ranchers are afraid to stay around here any longer."

"Then there should be plenty to choose from," Marge replied.

"Naturally, you would think so. However, the Big Sky Company, which is part of a large eastern corporation, has been buying up all land and buildings as soon as they come on the market."

"So, nothing is available?" she pressed him.

Jeff hesitated. "I've heard the Henderson family is moving out, since the old man was shot recently. But the Big Sky has a standing offer for any land and is paying fair market value. You could try and outbid the company, but from what I know they have pretty deep pockets and would simply keep raising the bid until you dropped out. I guess to answer your question, there really isn't anything available."

"How would Marge contact this company?" Brad asked.

"Oh, there's no way to talk to anyone there directly. I'm their local representative and have power of attorney to conduct all local real estate transactions. I send the company reports from time to time, depending on the level of activity, and keep them apprised of any land acquisitions. So any communication with them would have to go through me," Jeff concluded.

"Well, I'm sorry you haven't been able to help us," Marge said. "But it has been a pleasure meeting you. I hope to see you again sometime." With that farewell, she turned and motioned for Brad to follow her before he might change his mind about wringing additional information from the worthless jerk.

Stepping outside, Brad asked what she wanted to do next, and added, "I still think pistol whipping the son of a bitch would be a lot easier and faster than playing out this charade."

"Be patient, Brad. I think we should head back to your place and go over everything we know. When Jim gets back," Marge paused, "Maybe he'll have found out something else to help us."

As they headed back to the mining office to get their horses, she told Brad it would be interesting to look at the paperwork in Mr. William's office. "I think later we should break in after dark. By that time, the businesses will be closed and there should be plenty of noise coming from the saloon so we can go in there without being noticed."

As they walked up the street, Jeff watched them from his office window. When the two were out of sight, he went back and shoved some papers in the desk drawer. Locking it, he put the closed sign on the door and hurried over to the telegraph office.

"Good afternoon, Mr. Williams," the telegraph operator said, as Jeff walked through the front door. "Would you like to send a telegram?"

"No, I thought I would just come by and see if you were having a nice day," Jeff snapped. "Of course I want to send a telegram. Now shut up while I compose it." Writing out his message to Mr. Hartman, he stressed the phrase "with all possible speed". Handing it to the clerk, Jeff asked, "The lines are still up, aren't they?"

"Yes sir, they are." Reading the text of the message, the clerk looked up with a confused expression on his face. "Why would you want Mr. Hartman to send in Federal Marshals, Mr. Williams? I thought the last thing you wanted around here was the law?"

God, thought Jeff. So many things happening at once: Jacob had failed to make sure Marge and Jason were killed in the old house, Jim McClair hadn't been seen since yesterday, Brad was asking questions about the Big Sky Company, and now even a stupid clerk was questioning his decisions.

Sighing with exasperation, Jeff explained. "I have to move my timetable forward. I'm going to send Jacob to notify the gang to attack the mining company tomorrow and when Marge, Jim and the Johansen brothers are dead, I'll need to be able to control the town.

If I don't have Federal Marshals here to enforce the law, as I see it, then Wilson will send in his own posse. If that happens, he will know I'm responsible because I'll be the only one left. So, I'm going to use one arm of the law to stop another one. Does that meet with your approval?" he asked sarcastically.

"You're the boss, Mr. Williams. I was just puzzled, didn't mean to offend you."

As the clerk went back to his work, sulking, Jeff left to see if he could find Jacob over at the saloon. Things could still work out if the gang did their job fast, he thought, and if the Marshals arrived before Wilson could interfere. Reaching the saloon, he chuckled, thinking of playing two groups of lawmen against each other.

* * *

Jim was glad he had left early in the morning. He was well into the timberline before the sun came up, and only a few miners straggling up the hill had even seen him leave town. Hopefully, his absence would make someone nervous.

Mike had gone over the map with him last night, so he knew the general direction to take. Keeping just inside the tree line, he worked his way slowly on a north-westerly course.

He was several miles up the valley before the sun was high enough to see any distance with the telescope. Looking around for a vantage point, he spotted a rocky outcropping several hundred yards ahead.

After finding a location to ground hitch Whisper, in among some trees where the horse couldn't be seen, Jim took the surveyors telescope up to the ledge and settled in.

Smoothing a surface on the ground, he placed the short tripod in position and mounted the telescope to the base. Peering through the eyepiece, he was amazed how far a person could see through one of these things. It made sense though, considering the distances involved in surveying.

He slowly swept the scope across the valley, but didn't see anything. Starting over, he systematically covered the tree line ahead of him and across the valley. Then he scanned the lower foothills in all directions for any movement.

Not seeing anything again, Jim waited close to half an hour before repeating the process. This time he saw a faint wisp of smoke a couple miles ahead, on this side of the valley. He decided to work his way toward the smoke and investigate. Putting the tripod back in its' case, he mounted Whisper and continued on, staying inside the tree line so he couldn't be seen.

As he got closer, the smoke became visible to the naked eye. He rode through draws to make sure he never broke the skyline where he knew he would stand out like a sore thumb and gradually worked his way to a place where he could see the smoke coming from a small cabin. It was tucked up in a grove of pine trees near the mouth of a small canyon.

Halting Whisper, he took his regular field glasses and studied the cabin and surrounding sheds. There was a small corral with three horses in it, but no sign of anyone. Jim continued watching, until he finally saw a woman come out of the cabin and throw a pan of water over the side of the porch. She took a long look around and then went back inside.

Jim watched the place a while longer, but saw no sign of anyone else. Riding cautiously forward, even though the place looked harmless, he approached within forty feet and stopped. "Hello, the house," he called out.

A moment later, the woman stepped out on the porch. "Who are you, Mister, and what are you doing out here this early in the morning?"

Dismounting, Jim started to walk closer, leading Whisper. After only taking a few steps, the woman stopped him.

"That's far enough, Mister."

He was about to speak, when he saw a slight movement of her eyes. Hearing the sound of a rifle being cocked, he quickly reached for his gun, but froze when a voice yelled out from behind him.

"Don't make another move, Mister, or I'll kill you so fast, you'll be dead before you hit the ground."

Son of a bitch, Jim cursed to himself. He had fallen for the oldest trick in the book. While an unarmed, innocent looking person let him approach, someone else had flanked him.

Slowly taking his hand from his gun, Jim turned. He was surprised to see a strikingly beautiful young woman holding a carbine. The barrel was pointed directly at his chest and from this distance there was no way she could miss.

He noticed the woman was confident and poised, with no fear in her eyes. Holding his hands up, he said, "I don't mean any harm, ladies."

"Maybe, maybe not," the one with the rifle said. "But you best explain your presence, and can start by answering my mother's questions."

He turned back to the woman on the porch, "My name's Jim McClair, and I was heading north when I spotted smoke and decided to check it out."

"If you're heading north, then you must be a rider for the Rocking Chair P ranch."

"No Ma'am. I'm out here investigating the shootings that have been occurring in the valley this year."

Hearing these words, the woman felt the man was no longer a danger and motioned her daughter to come forward. "You might as well sit on the porch and we'll talk up here. Can I get you a cup of coffee?"

"That would be wonderful, thank you."

When the three of them had settled down in some old wooden chairs, he took a big gulp of coffee and then rolled a cigarette. Lighting it and exhaling a cloud of smoke, he looked at the two women, "I didn't mean to frighten you this morning."

The woman smiled and looked at her daughter for a second. "Mister McClair, we don't frighten, and my daughter could put a bullet between your eyes at a hundred paces if she wanted to. And if you had made a threatening move, I would have stepped back inside where I keep a loaded shotgun next to the door. So you see," she said laughing, "If you had known, you would have been scared of us."

"Don't you think you should introduce us, Ma?" the daughter interrupted, as she smiled at the handsome stranger who had broken up their dull morning routine.

"I'm sorry. Where are my manners? My name is Laurie and this is my daughter, Lisa. We've lived out here for years and I forget that strangers don't know who we are."

As Jim looked around at the homestead, Laurie spoke up, "It doesn't seem like much and we've never had a lot, but it's been comfortable, and a place we could call home. Of course, now that Lisa is getting old enough to think of other things, she has the desire to move to a big city."

"Mom, there's no men out here for a young woman, except some smelly cowboys or dirty miners. I have to go where I can meet exciting people, and do something besides cook and clean all day."

Jim smiled at the thought of her youthful dreams, and then turned back to Laurie. "Where is your husband?"

"He was one of the first victims of the shooter this spring," she stated matter-of-factly.

"I'm sorry to hear that. I understand other families moved out of the area after a family member got killed. If you don't mind me asking, what made you decide to stay?'"

"I was very upset, and angry at first, when Steve was killed, because I loved him and we had a pretty good marriage. The only real problem we had was whenever there were a few dollars set aside; he would go into town and throw it away on gambling and drinking.

However, I've always been a practical woman, and after the initial shock wore off; I realized keeping our homestead going was a lot easier with him gone."

Not sure how to respond to such a blunt assessment, Jim asked her if they were going to continue staying here alone.

"Well, I plan on staying here, though I don't know if it will be by myself after Lisa moves on. You never know, maybe someday I'll meet a man worth keeping." Glancing at her daughter, who was blushing now, Laurie continued, "but I'm not going to sit around pining away for a man to make my life complete."

Jim tried to keep from laughing, and knowing he still had many miles to cover, changed the subject. "How close am I to the Rocking Chair range?"

Laurie thought for a moment, "Their boundary is about three or four miles from here. You can't miss it, because signs are posted every quarter mile warning people to stay off. But I've never heard of anyone getting shot up there."

"That's exactly why I'm going on their land. It makes me a little suspicious," Jim said.

"I see what you mean. I never gave it any thought before, because I figured the ranch had enough cowboys and gunhands to scare the shooter away."

"Well, that may be, but I had better get moving and check it out," Jim said, as he finished his coffee. Before leaving, he warned the women to be extra careful, because if the situation in the valley got stirred up, things could get pretty ugly.

Thanking him for his concern, the two women watched as he mounted Whisper and rode back into the tree line.

As Laurie stared at him riding away, Lisa nudged her in the side, "See Ma, there are men worth taking a second look at."

Pretending to be annoyed, she scolded Lisa. "Don't talk like that. Now go do some of those chores you're always complaining about."

Giggling, Lisa headed back to the barn to feed the horses.

* * *

Jim stayed concealed in the tree line as he worked his way in the direction of the Rocking Chair range. He rode carefully so he wouldn't expose himself to anyone who might be watching for movement. Coming down a slope, he noticed there was a small wagon trail that led through the forest. Curious, he followed the tracks as they meandered among the trees and headed into the mouth of a narrow canyon.

The stand of Poplars began to thin and he stopped to study the land in front of him. What he had thought was just another tree filled canyon, turned out to be a couple hundred acres of grazing land.

Taking his field glasses, Jim looked for any signs of people. He couldn't see anyone and was surprised there weren't any cattle being kept in here. Continuing his search with the glasses, he finally spotted a log cabin located in the far left corner of the box canyon.

From where he was the cabin looked deserted. He didn't see any smoke, or horses outside, and the trail cutting across the grass didn't look like it had been used in a long time. Satisfied that no one was around, he rode across the field. About half way to the cabin he came to a small creek running through the property.

It was maybe ten feet wide and when Whisper stepped into it, he could see the water was almost a foot deep. Riding up on the other side of the bank, he turned and looked at the field again.

This place was absolutely serene. The meadow was broken up with stands of Alders and Poplars, and along the creek were chokecherry trees and other small bushes. The entire place had a relaxed, peaceful feeling about it.

173

Turning Whisper, Jim continued riding in the direction of the cabin. He approached with caution, even though there was no sign of anyone. Bringing his horse to a halt by a large tree, he took a closer look at it.

The log cabin was a one story building, with a high peaked roof. Now that he was closer, he could see it was quite large. There was a porch running the entire length of the front, and on both ends of the cabin were stone chimneys.

This cabin had obviously been built by a craftsman, because the logs had been carefully selected and put together in such a way that it looked like a real home, rather than just some place to live in.

While he was admiring the quality of the construction, he noticed a sign on the front door. Dismounting, he walked onto the porch and read the paper that had been nailed there. In big black letters, it read, "PRIVATE PROPERTY...NO TRESPASSING! THE BIG SKY COMPANY".

When he got back to town, he would have to locate the company and find out what their plans were for this piece of property. He liked the privacy of the home and could imagine living here if the place was for sale. After taking one last look around, he mounted Whisper and headed back towards the mouth of the canyon.

Continuing to ride in a northwesterly direction, he came to a bluff. Deciding this would be a good place to take another look around; he worked his way up through the trees and found a spot to ground hitch Whisper.

Taking the telescope, and keeping low, Jim worked his way to the edge of the cliff. Setting up his tripod and mounting the scope, he began surveying the valley from this new vantage point.

From here he could see cowboys working some cattle toward a river where the main herd appeared to be gathered. None of the riders seemed to be worried about being in the open during daylight hours. He thought this was a little strange, considering how paranoid everyone else was about getting caught in the open with a shooter on the loose.

Rotating the scope so that he had a view of the other side of the valley, he slowly studied the tree line and then any high points. He knew if a sniper was out here, the person would be concealed in a place much like he was. After a thorough search, and not seeing anything suspicious, he draped a cloth over the scope and relaxed.

He couldn't look continuously through the scope for a couple of reasons. One, his eyes would get tired and the odds were he would miss some motion, or glint of light off glass or metal. Another was that someone might be looking through their own field glasses and catch a reflection off the scope Jim was using.

Checking his watch, he noticed a half hour had gone by. Uncovering the scope, he did another search of the far side of the valley. Not seeing anything again, he decided to swing the scope from north to south one more time before taking a break.

As he moved the glasses across a jumble of rocks on a wooded slope, he caught a quick flash of sunlight reflecting off a surface. He quickly covered his scope in case it was a person over there. After a few minutes, he slowly pulled the cloth up just enough so he could see through the lens.

Focusing on the place where the reflection had been seen, he studied the area. He knew if a person was over there they would not be sky lined, so he looked at the

175

edge of rocks or trees for any signs. Near a large boulder, in front of a stand of trees, he was finally rewarded. There was a rifle lying on the ground.

The barrel was pointed slightly upward, and it puzzled Jim for a second until he realized the front of the barrel was resting on a small log. Whoever was over there must have left the butt of the rifle on the ground.

After about ten minutes of watching, and not seeing anyone, Jim surveyed the valley again. Nothing unusual was going on down there, so he covered the scope and rested.

On the second or third time he checked out the rocks, he was rewarded with a view of the person waiting there.

The man had cautiously stepped out from behind a tree and picked up the rifle. He appeared to be about thirty, with a handle bar mustache, and instead of a typical western hat, he had a bandana tied around his forehead. Jim could also tell the person was short and slender. Unfortunately, a person didn't have to be a big man; physically, or emotionally to pull a trigger.

The man set the rifle back down and lifted up a pair of field glasses. Since Jim was on a slight angle behind the area where the man was looking, he was no longer worried about being seen.

Studying the man in the rocks, Jim couldn't help but smile to himself, thinking about him watching the watcher. Jim's mood turned serious again when the man put down the glasses and picked up his rifle and placed it in a firing position across a rock.

Jim swung his telescope towards the direction the man's rifle was pointed and could see a cowboy slowly riding out of a ravine. Tensing at what he thought was about to happen, and too far away to do anything about it, Jim was surprised when the cowboy stopped and tied a red cloth to his saddle horn.

Getting suspicious now, Jim turned his telescope back to the shooter in the rocks and saw that he had lowered his rifle. The red cloth must have been a signal not to shoot. So that was part of the game these bastards were playing here on the Rocking Chair P range.

As far as Jim was concerned, he had seen enough to accept the man in the rocks as the shooter who was killing innocent people in the valley.

There was no direct evidence that would stand up in a court of law. However, with the shootings that had occurred during the summer and this man waiting patiently with a rifle, along with the red flag incident he had just witnessed, Jim considered the circumstantial evidence too much to ignore.

Having made up his mind to accept the man in the rocks as the sniper, Jim realized he had another problem. The surveyor's telescope had worked wonders at seeing across the valley, but now he had to physically move through the valley without being seen by the cowboys working the herd, or by the person in the rocks.

Studying the terrain, he noticed there were trees lining both sides of the river. Except for occasional places where grass went up to the water's edge, he should be able to work his way to the other side of the valley without being seen by anyone. Unfortunately, the silhouette of a man astride a horse would be too obvious, so he would have to walk next to his horse through the trees.

Jim followed the river with his glasses and estimated that he would come out about a mile north of where the shooter had been spotted.

After a route had been decided on, he went back for

177

Whisper and rode down the slope. On this side of the valley the forest extended out to the river, so he was able to ride that far. Once there, he dismounted and began walking. Keeping Whisper between himself and the shooter, Jim worked his way among the trees.

Jim figured it would probably take quite a while to reach the other side. However, in this kind of game, patience was not only a virtue…it could mean the difference between life and death.

When Jim reached the occasional break in the trees, he would stay close to the front of Whisper and walk slowly across the opening. Most people would rush across the exposed area as quickly as possible. However, he knew sudden movements were more likely to catch the eye of someone watching than slow motion would.

It seemed like forever, but eventually he came to the woods on the far side of the valley and was able to ride Whisper again.

Having a good sense of direction, Jim began working his way up the slope and looking for a safe observation point. Several hundred yards to the south, and on his left, was a thick stand of trees on a knoll.

As he was approaching the back side of it, Jim heard three evenly spaced shots from the valley. Quickly riding into the cluster of Poplar trees, he dismounted and considered the shots. Three in a row usually meant a call for help, but in this case it was probably a warning.

Assuming the worst; that he had been seen by a cowboy down by the herd, Jim tied Whisper to a low branch and got out his field glasses.

Stepping to the edge of the trees, he scanned the area around the cattle. Sure enough, one of the riders was looking up in his general direction. Shortly, the cowboy stopped staring at the hillside and went back to the herd.

Jim knew he would have to now operate under the assumption that the shooter would be looking for an unknown person in the surrounding area. Well, the element of surprise wasn't completely lost. The shooter had no idea who, or where Jim was; only that someone was around.

Checking to make sure his rifle and revolver were fully loaded, Jim untied the long wooden case from his horse. Leaving the surveyor's telescope behind, he carried the case with him as he carefully moved through the trees. Eventually, he found a good field of vision in the direction of where he had last seen the shooter.

Keeping his movements slow and deliberate, Jim took his knife and trimmed off two forked branches and placed them in the ground about two feet apart. After setting a stick across the forks, he collected a small pile of branches. Carefully, he placed these over the cross piece. Scattering several handfuls of leaves over the top of this, he stood back and studied his handiwork. The canopy made it difficult for anyone to see him, but the open space below provided a small opening for him to look through.

Satisfied with the makeshift blind, Jim went back to the case and unlocked it. Raising the lid, he looked at the weapon tied down inside. The rifle was a specially modified 45-90, with a custom made barrel that was six inches longer than the standard issue.

The gunsmith had also modified the trigger assembly. Now there were two triggers; the first for taking up the initial slack of the firing mechanism, and the second, for a smooth release of the firing pin.

Mounted on top was the most advanced scope he

could purchase at the time, and at the front of the rifle the gunsmith had attached a swivel bipod to the barrel. This allowed Jim to have a stable resting place without having to find a rock or log to set the barrel on.

A cartridge belt had been screwed into the side of the case and held twenty bullets. Each cartridge had been hand loaded by the same gunsmith and had extra gun powder for firing extremely long distances.

Jim smiled to himself and thought about the three banks he had accounts in. No one knew that in the safety deposit boxes he had at their banks, he had placed one hundred rounds each. If anything happened to him, there would certainly be a lot of head scratching when those boxes were eventually opened.

Bringing his attention back to the present, Jim considered the shot he would have to make. His best estimate of the distance for this target was just under three quarters of a mile. However, he had practiced with over two hundred rounds and knew he could hit a target, comfortably, from a mile away.

Feeling confident in his abilities, Jim lifted up the rifle and worked the bolt into the rear position. Placing a cartridge into the chamber and sliding the bolt home, he then put two more rounds in his shirt pocket.

Returning to the canopy, Jim lowered himself to the ground. Folding down the bipod legs, he settled into position and used the scope on his rifle to begin searching for the location of the shooter.

Scanning the area, Jim finally saw the dead pine tree that he knew was close to where the shooter had been earlier. After looking for several minutes and not seeing anything, he let go of the rifle and closed his eyes. He knew that trying to watch for extended periods of time would irritate them and make his vision blurry, so his plan was to alternate between searching the area for a few minutes and resting his eyes.

Jim had time to continue the internal debate during the rest periods, about what he was doing. He knew the law would not condone his plan of action...even though he had been deputized by Wilson. And the court system and lawyers would certainly have a fit, knowing all the evidence in front of him was circumstantial.

On the other hand, he reminded himself, numerous people had fallen victim to a mysterious shooter. And, from what Jim had observed from the other side of the valley, the person obviously wasn't up there protecting the cattle herd. So as far as Jim was concerned, the evidence was good enough for applying a little common sense and some frontier justice.

About forty five minutes later, Jim finally spotted a glimpse of the bandana the shooter was wearing. The man was motionless for awhile, and then he stepped a little farther out from behind a rock.

Jim slowly squeezed the first trigger, which took up the slack in the firing mechanism, and gently exhaled as he lined up the cross hairs in the scope on the man's shoulder.

Suddenly, instead of edging into the open a little further where Jim could take a shot, the man darted across the opening and disappeared behind a rock.

Damn, Jim thought. So close! Lowering his head to relax his eyes for a moment, his thoughts drifted back to the War.

How many men had died by his hand? He had never kept track like so many of the snipers did, and Jim had personally found it offensive that anyone could count the

181

bodies like they were trophy's of some sort. If you had to take a life, it should be because of the situation you were in (like war) or because the person deserved killing.

As Jim started dwelling on the numerous atrocities that he had seen committed, not because of sound military strategy, but because of petty emotions; or worse yet, for monetary gain...The sound of a squirrel chattering nearby brought his attentions back to the present.

Lifting the butt of the rifle back up to his shoulder, Jim again started scanning the trees and rocks. Every so often, he would catch a glimpse of the shooter as he moved stealthily from one cover to another. It was obvious the man was concerned that he could not locate the person he had been warned about with the three shots.

Jim noticed the man was working his way towards a cluster of pine trees near a large boulder. Moving the rifle slightly, so that he could study the area near the trees, Jim saw a spot where the shooter would be exposed for several feet.

It was already mid-afternoon and Jim could not afford to let darkness fall. If that happened, the shooter would be gone and who knew where he would show up tomorrow. The small window of opportunity offered by the few feet of open space would have to be the time for him to attempt to kill the man.

Making quick approximations in his mind about the distance involved, and the slight breeze blowing, Jim sighted the cross hairs in the scope on a small branch that was about chest high. The spot also gave Jim about a four foot lead, which he needed because he knew the man would sprint across the opening.

Observing the advance of the shooter from the corner

of his eye, Jim slowly exhaled and placed his finger on the second trigger.

The moment Jim caught the flash of movement from the shooter entering the clearing, he squeezed the trigger.

The tremendous noise, and recoil of the rifle firing caused the makeshift canopy to collapse on him. Leaving his rifle there for the moment, Jim jumped up and brushed the twigs off his head and face. Grabbing his field glasses, he looked across to where he had fired.

With grim satisfaction, he saw the man sprawled on the ground. The high velocity round had caught the man in the right chest and slammed him into a rock; Jim could see a bright smear of blood on a rock just behind the man.

Stepping out where he could look down into the valley, Jim turned his glasses to the herd of cattle. A couple of the cowhands were looking up in his general direction, but the rest of them were going about their business like nothing had happened.

This just confirmed Jim's suspicions that the ranch hands knew about the shooter. No wonder nobody had ever been shot from the Rocking Chair P.

Relieved that no one was heading up the slope to check things out, Jim cleaned off his sniper rifle and put it back in the case.

Mounting Whisper, he began working his way over to the fallen man. Pausing every few minutes, and studying the scene with his glasses, Jim got closer and finally stopped and dismounted.

Leading Whisper, Jim cautiously scouted the area while approaching the shooter. When he finally reached the dead man, he turned him over. He could see where the bullet had exited the man's left side, leaving a hole as big as a fist, and he knew the man had died without ever understanding what had happened.

Searching the man's pockets, Jim found a wad of bills, but no identification. There must be several hundred dollars he figured. In a vest pocket, he found a map of the area.

Smoothing out the map, he studied it. Noticing red check marks by numerous properties, he realized the marks represented farms and ranches that had been a target of the sniper. He found the deserted place he had admired a few hours ago. Sure enough, there was a red check by it.

Moving his finger along the route he had taken, Jim soon found the small farm where Laurie and Lisa lived. There was a red mark here also, but next to it was a question mark. This must be because Laurie had not sold out like everyone else. He folded the map and placed it in his pocket. Wilson would want to see this eventually.

Walking over to where the man's rifle was laying on the ground, he looked at it. The rifle was a sharp's .50, a deadly, long range weapon for anyone who knew what they were doing.

Curious as to where the sniper had been staying at night, Jim scouted around for sign and soon found a trail that led through the trees. Having no sympathy for the dead sniper, he decided coyotes and other wild animals would take care of the body, so he mounted Whisper and began following the path.

Staying alert for any signs of people, he worked his way across three or four miles of wooded canyons and hills. The sniper had obviously been using the same trail to enter the main valley, because the path showed steady use. Coming to the top of another hill, he dismounted and walked cautiously forward.

Stepping up behind a tree, Jim could see into the next canyon without being visible himself. He was surprised to see a small meadow with a large group of men standing around campfires.

After getting his field glasses, Jim studied the men below. They appeared to be passing bottles of whiskey around, and not doing anything else except smoking and talking. As he swept his glasses across one campfire, he froze. There were the men who had planned on raping Marge back at the way station.

Suppressing the urge to take his rifle and start killing the bastards, he calmed down by counting them. As near as he could tell, there were thirty seven scattered around the meadow. What this large number of men were doing out here in the middle of nowhere was puzzling, so he decided to observe the camp for a while before heading back.

As the afternoon dragged on, the men became drunker and louder. He was to far away to make out what anyone was talking about, but he had at least identified the person who seemed to be in charge.

The man carried himself with a military bearing and looked to be about Jim's size. While the man took a sip from a bottle occasionally, Jim noticed that he never had enough to get drunk. He obviously had enough self control to make sure he stayed in command of what appeared to be an outlaw army.

Jim debated whether he should simply go ahead and shoot the leader, which would take care of any organizational control. As he was contemplating the risks involved, namely, how the hell he would get away from a group of men this large, a horse came galloping up through another entrance to the meadow.

Apparently the men recognized the rider, because after a tense moment when they heard the horse approaching, they relaxed and went back to drinking.

The rider pulled his horse to a halt in front of the leader and dismounted. The man looked physically like half the men down there, but when he approached the leader and took off his hat, Jim could see the man's face was pock marked. Filing the description away for future reference, he continued to watch.

There was no way to hear what was said, but shortly after arriving the man got back on his horse and left. As soon as he had ridden off, the leader began barking out orders. Jim watched as everyone started checking and cleaning their weapons. When this was done, each man went to their horse and got ready for traveling.

Jim didn't know what all the commotion was about, but he knew it was getting late and he couldn't afford to get caught up here. Quietly moving back to Whisper, he mounted and rode back up the trail he had followed to this point.

Returning to the location of the dead shooter, Jim took his field glasses and checked out the herd in the valley. The work must be done for the day, because there were only two cowhands keeping an eye on the cattle.

Since dusk was settling in, and he didn't have to worry about a shooter in the hills anymore, he decided it would be safe to simply ride back down along the river bank.

Crossing the valley, Jim rode towards Laurie's place. Approaching the cabin, he saw the light from a lantern coming from the front window. Shouting to the cabin, he noticed quick movement from within. He knew Lisa was probably flanking him, so he just relaxed while he waited for an answer from the cabin.

After a few moments, the front door cracked open, and Laurie yelled, "Who's out there?"

"It's me," Jim yelled.

Recognizing his voice, she relaxed. Calling into the darkness for Lisa to come on in, she told him to hitch his horse.

When they were all inside and relaxing with a cup of coffee, he told them about the days events. Rolling a smoke, he explained about the outlaws getting ready to travel and warned them to move away from the house before sunup. "I don't know if they'll even pass by here, but the safest thing you can do is to hide in the hills and wait until they leave."

After making sure they understood the seriousness of the situation, he thanked Laurie for the coffee and rode Whisper out into the valley. Riding fast, now that he was in the open, Jim reached the Johansen place before midnight.

* * *

As he rode toward the barn, Jim noticed the house was lit up. Probably another party going on, he mused. After putting Whisper in a stall and rubbing him down, he took the rifle case and went up the porch steps. Since there seemed to be a lot of noise coming from inside the house, he didn't bother knocking.

He could hear a discussion going on in the parlor, so he slipped quietly up the stairs to put away his rifle. After changing into a clean pair of jeans and a fresh shirt, he washed his face and combed his hair. Feeling somewhat refreshed, he grabbed a pouch of tobacco and headed downstairs.

As Jim entered the parlor, Mike was the first to see him. "Where the hell have you been? You don't look like you've been up in the hills all day."

Before he could answer, Marge came running up and threw her arms around him. "Oh Jim, I'm so glad you made it back," as she gave him a passionate kiss.

After giving her an equally passionate kiss back, he looked up at the men standing around grinning at him. Feeling himself getting a little flushed, he released her. "Before I tell you what I've found out and accomplished, could someone bring me a whiskey?"

David went to get him a drink while the rest of them settled down in chairs scattered in front of a roaring blaze in the fireplace.

"We have quite a bit to tell you also, Jim," Marge said. "But let's hear about your day first, okay?"

Thanking David for the drink and taking a sip, Jim summarized the day's adventure. When he got to the part about a man riding hard into the outlaw camp, Justin

188

interrupted.

"That has to be Jacob you described. He's the bastard who sent two men around to kill Jason and Marge."

A cold shiver went down Jim's spine as he gripped Marge's hand. "Maybe someone better tell me what happened around here today!"

Marge looked at Brad and Jason. Nodding their heads for her to tell the story, she began by describing how they had found the secret tunnel to the mining office vault, and then mentioned they had left the entrance in the old mansion undisturbed.

"Wait a minute," Jim said, as he held up his hand. "You purposely left the entrance available for someone else to go in and grab more gold?"

"It sounds worse than it is," Jason spoke up. "Justin kept an eye on the place all afternoon, and tonight he has another man back in the woods. He didn't tell the man what was happening, just to let us know immediately if anyone went into the house."

"Let's get back to this Jacob?" Jim asked. You said he sent men to kill the two of you?"

Brad cleared his throat, "It wasn't Jacob who sent the men. We believe it was Jeff Williams who ordered Jacob to go and find men who were willing to kill on a moments notice. Jacob was just the errand boy, and from what you've told us, he was given another message to deliver to the outlaw gang. The fact that the gang was getting ready to ride worries me more than Jacob's role in this."

"It does me too," Jim said. Pausing to roll a smoke, he continued, "But I'd like to hear more about Jeff Williams first, what do we know about him?"

Mike started laughing, "A hell of a lot more than we

ever imagined. Everybody in town thought he was just a small town lawyer who ran the Land and Title Company. Little did we know...?"

Marge waved Mike into silence, "This is just too funny. Please, let me tell Jim about our adventure tonight." Grinning, Mike leaned back and lit a cigar.

After finishing off her glass of scotch, Marge accepted a cigarette from Brad and explained. "When Brad asked Jeff how I could get in touch with the Big Sky Company, Jeff told us that would be impossible. According to Jeff, all contacts had to be made through him. That seemed kind of strange to us, so we made plans to break into his office after dark."

As Jim's eyes narrowed, she hastily added, "We left Justin and David in the back alley for protection, and to stop anyone from snooping around and noticing us."

Nodding his head in approval, Jim asked, "From the excitement on everyone's face, I presume you found something?"

"More than we could have hoped for," she replied. "We carefully jimmied the locks on the drawers so when Jeff opens up tomorrow he won't know we've been in there, and started going through the contents. Anyway, we found a file containing paperwork for the Big Sky Company. Guess who owns it?" she asked excitedly.

Puzzled, Jim looked around at everyone grinning. "I haven't a clue."

"Jeff Williams! That's who."

Jim shook his head. "I don't understand."

"We didn't at first, either," Brad said. "However, after looking through more papers, we realized that Jeff "is" the Big Sky Company! There is no eastern corporation buying up land around here."

Marge squeezed Jim's hand. "Don't you see? Jeff has been buying all the land coming up for sale. Since everyone knew the Big Sky Company had a standing offer to pay a fair price for any land, then he has to be the one who hired the shooter to scare off families."

"Yeah," Mike interrupted, "and the son of a bitch was probably using our gold to buy it. Talk about adding insult to injury. It looks like Jeff was planning on taking over the entire valley and we would be financing it!"

Jim lit a cigarette, and leaned back with a smile on his face.

"What do you find so amusing about that?" Jason asked. "Both you and Marge seem to get a kick out of our troubles around here."

Exhaling, Jim shook his head, "It's not that we find your problems funny, and we certainly feel bad about all the killings that have taken place. However, a person has to admire the sheer audacity of the plan. Also, think of the creative planning and control it must have taken to keep this operation going...and quiet? But you must realize of course, that ultimately Jeff would need to make a move on the mine itself?"

"That's one of the things we were discussing this evening," Brad said, "and now that you've told us about the gang getting ready to ride, the attack is probably going to happen real soon. So what are we going to do about it?"

"Well," Jim replied. "The gang is big enough to split into groups. I think they'll send a small one through the other end of town as a diversion, and the main body of men will probably sneak back through the same canyon I followed into the valley. What we need to do is have a surprise party waiting for them. What else would you suggest we do, Marge?"

"With all the planning Jeff has put into this operation, I'm sure he'll send a few men to take the rest of the gold just in case things go wrong with the gang taking over. I would put some men down in the vault, and I'd do it before daylight."

I'll get a few men I trust and go down there," David volunteered. "I'll need to get the keys though. Is there anything I should tell the guard who's on duty?"

Jason handed over his keys. "Don't tell him anything. In fact, take him downstairs with you so we don't have to worry about any loose talk accidentally tipping off Jeff. Make sure all the men have shotguns."

After David left, Mike asked if there was anything he and Justin should do.

"I think Jim's hunch is correct about part of the gang coming through the ravine running up to the back of the mine," Brad said. "Why don't you and Justin take several men up there before sunrise and position yourselves along both sides of it. Take along plenty of ammunition."

"What about the people in town?" Jason asked, concerned. "Shouldn't they be alerted to a possible attack?"

"They don't need to be warned!" Jim stated bluntly. "With the first sound of gunfire they'll either stand and fight, or hide. It's more important we keep the element of surprise."

After a debate about the merits of warning, or defending the town, there was a general agreement that the town was not the real target. Consequently, people there could fend for themselves while the mining company did their best to stop the gang. If the outlaws could be stopped, then Jeff Williams would be dealt with afterwards.

It was decided that Brad and Jason would take up a position between the buildings across from the mine headquarters, Marge would stay at the house, and Jim would keep an eye on the Land & Title Company.

Once these decisions had been made, Jim suggested they all try to get a few hours sleep. "Since we can't afford to get a late start in the morning, I'll stay up for awhile and then wake you or Jason. Okay?"

Everyone was too keyed up to sleep, but they nodded in agreement, realizing even a short rest could make a big difference in the morning.

When the other men had left, Marge reached out for Jim's hand. "I was so worried, knowing what you were doing out in the valley. Were you in danger?"

Jim leaned over and kissed her lightly on the lips. "The most dangerous time was when I found the outlaw gang. I was lucky they didn't have sentries out. If they had, there wouldn't have been any way to out run that many men."

Giving her hand a squeeze, he continued. "We're fine right now, and if we make it through tomorrow I'd like to show you a place I found out in the valley."

Listening to his description of the beautiful log cabin located in a stand of Poplar and Pine trees, her eyes lit up. "The place sounds so beautiful and peaceful, Jim. I'd love to see it."

"That reminds me, Jim. When you mentioned finding the "no trespassing" sign on the cabin door from the Big Sky Company, I forgot to tell you about another file we came across in Jeff William's desk. He has a whole stack of quit claim deeds from the properties he bought, but he never took them to Helena and filed the paperwork at the County Courthouse."

"I guess Jeff figured there was plenty of time to take care of that later on," Jim reflected. "When we do finally have a talk with him, maybe it's something we can use?"

After visiting for a while, Marge became sleepy and curled up on the couch next to Jim. When she fell asleep on his shoulder, he gently moved her aside and stood up. Finding a blanket in a closet he gently covered her. Rolling a smoke, he turned the lantern down low and went out on the porch.

The morning would be here before he knew it, and there were many facts and speculations to consider. Jim could never forget the long sleepless hours under battlefield conditions, and knew he would stay awake the rest of the night and let everyone else sleep as long as possible.

About four in the morning, he gently shook Marge awake. "It's time to get up."

Stirring, she groaned, "What an ungodly hour to be woken."

"I'll put a pot of coffee on and wake Jason and Brad while you freshen up." Walking upstairs, he knocked on their doors and then went back to the kitchen. The coffee wasn't as hot as he liked, but it would do. Pouring a cup for Marge and himself, he brought one to her.

"Well, thank God for small favors," as she gratefully accepted the cup. After taking a drink of coffee, she asked, "When are you going into town, Jim?"

"I want to be down in the alley before sunrise, but first I'm going to make sure you have several weapons available." Hearing the sound of the men coming down the stairs, he quickly leaned over and gave her a kiss.

"That's a nice way to start the morning," she said with a smile. "What's that for?"

"I just wanted you to know I'll be thinking of you," he smiled back. "You be careful today and don't show any mercy if you're attacked."

"Don't worry about me. You just watch your back!"

Moments later, Brad and Jason walked into the parlor. "I thought you were going to wake one of us?" Brad asked.

"Sorry, I was too wound up," Jim replied. "I'm ready to head into town, but I wanted to make sure Marge had some guns handy before I left."

Walking over to a cabinet, Jason took out a shotgun. "Is this too big for you, Marge?"

"That'll do just fine. I'll also put one rifle inside the parlor door and my rifle upstairs in case I have to retreat. Plus, I'll have my derringer on me. I think I can defend the house if it's attacked."

While they went over the general plan one more time, Jim made sure his colt had six rounds in the chamber and his rifle was fully loaded. Saying goodbye, he left and headed for town.

He didn't want to be noticed, so he left Whisper in the stable and walked briskly. Staying close to buildings he soon came to the alley behind the Land & Title Company. He found a pile of crates where he could wait without being seen by any other early risers and settling in, he began the patient wait for sunrise.

*

The guard at the mining office was surprised when David showed up in the middle of the night with several armed men. He was even more shocked when David opened the door. Nobody ever had the keys except the brothers. "What the hell is going on?" he asked.

"We're going down in the vault and wait there," David replied. "Leave your lantern on and follow us. Other than that, I can't tell you what we're waiting for, or what might happen."

Confused, but not willing to argue with the lead foreman, the guard grabbed his shotgun and went down in the vault with the other men.

Setting his lantern on top of a box of gold, David turned to the men. "If any of you want to rest, go ahead. Otherwise, I think it's okay to smoke down here and I brought a deck of cards if anyone wants to play poker while we wait."

"Some friendly poker sounds good to me," one of the men said. "But what will we use for money?"

David smiled and held up the key ring. "We'll probably never be rich men ourselves, but for a few hours we can pretend we are." Finding the right key, he began opening several boxes of gold. "Let's each start with ten bars. One bar to ante up and a two bar limit on the bet. How does that sound?"

The men began laughing as they set up empty boxes to sit on and settled in for some high stakes poker.

"Wait until I tell the boys down at the saloon about this," one man chuckled.

"Hell, they'll never believe you," another man laughed.

*

With a lot of grumbling and cussing, Mike and Justin rousted half a dozen miners they could count on, and told them to bring their rifles and plenty of ammunition. While the men got ready, Justin got the fire in the stove going and put on a pot of coffee.

"Do you know it's the middle of the night, Mike?" a man complained as he put on his boots.

"It'll be sunrise in a couple hours Harry, so don't start any bitching. I don't want to be out here any more than you do."

As men rolled smokes and poured themselves cups of coffee, Mike explained where they were going and what the plan was.

"You mean we're going to walk all the way to the canyon?" someone asked.

"It's not even half a mile," Justin said. "Besides, we can't afford to have the horses make any noise and alert the gang. Hell, we don't even know if they'll show up. If they don't, each of you will get ten dollars and the next two days off. Does that sound fair?"

Hearing this, the mood of the men brightened considerably. "Come on men," Harry said. "Let's get walking. We either have us a turkey shoot, or a two day party."

"That's the spirit," Mike said. Finishing their coffee, the men followed Mike and Justin out the door and toward the canyon.

*

Leaving Marge at the house, Brad and Jason headed toward the mine office. As they walked along, Brad asked, "Do you think she'll be okay by herself?"

Jason chuckled, "If you had seen how calm and deadly she was down in the basement of the old mansion, you wouldn't be asking. That'll be a story worth telling over again."

Seeing the mine headquarters up ahead, Brad pointed to an opening between two vacant buildings. "That looks like a good place to wait."

By now, the first light of day was just coming over the eastern mountains, and the sounds of early activity could be heard from farther in town.

"Well, we might as well make ourselves comfortable and settle in for the wait," Brad said, as he rolled a cigarette.

Lighting a cigar for himself, Jason exhaled a cloud of smoke. "You know, waiting like this reminds me of our hunting trips. If we get things taken care of around here, and make it through," he added, "Let's go on a hunt this fall. I'd love to get away from the mines again."

Brad smiled at his brother, "That does sound fun, and relaxing. It has been a long time."

After a little kidding around, they leaned back and enjoyed the quiet company of each other while waiting for something to happen.

* * *

The gang had made a cold camp about three miles from town and as the sun began to rise, their leader, Walt, went around and woke everyone up. "Check your weapons and get your horses saddled," he called out.

When the men were ready, they gathered around him. "Here's my plan. I want a dozen men to ride with Jake and circle around to the east side of town. There's a stand of trees down by the river where you can wait.

At seven o'clock…your watch still work, Jake?" Jake checked his pocket watch and nodded. "As I was saying, at seven o'clock I want his group to ride into town and start shooting the place up. Make as much noise as possible and feel free to shoot anyone who gets in your way. I want a lot of panic.

As soon as you reach the town, I want four men to cut behind the buildings and make their way to the Johansen house. Make sure you kill anyone there."

"Hey Walt?" a man asked.

"What is it, Leo?"

"Jacob said the woman I told you about, the one who backed us down at the way station, is staying at their house. Can me and my boys be the ones to hit it? We have a personal score to settle with that bitch."

Walt smiled to himself. A little vengeance and anger always made men fight more eagerly. "That's okay with me."

"Now," Walt continued, "While Jake is creating a diversion, the rest of us will come through the canyon on the back side of the mine. Once we're there, I'll send Matt and five men to the old mansion. Their job will be to go down and remove the rest of the gold from the

199

vault.

The men staying with me will disarm, or kill, anyone who tries to stop us. Remember, the Johansen brothers have to die. Any questions"

"How are we going to have time to move all that gold?" Matt asked.

"I don't want the gold brought back up, because it would take too long. All I want you to do is set it in the tunnel and close the wall. We'll come back later and get it. If anything goes wrong, I want to make sure we're well paid for sitting around in the mountains these last few weeks. Now, is there anything else?"

As some of the men topped off their coffee with shots of whiskey and started talking about what they would do with their share, another man spoke up. "Leroy never came back to camp last night."

"Don't worry about him," Walt replied. "Those snipers are a strange breed. He probably decided to spend the night where he keeps an eye on the valley. If that's all, then pick the rest of your men, Jake, and get into position."

After saddling up, Jake and his men rode off. Walt checked his watch and told everyone to have another cup of coffee and a smoke. "Then we're going to finish our job here and get paid one way or another."

Amid the laughter, there was the usual nervous tension that was created whenever men headed into a violent confrontation. Everyone was keyed up and checked their rifles and hand guns a second time before Walt told them to mount up and follow him.

As the men spread out in a loose group, they rode silently across the valley. It was just a few minutes before seven when they approached the narrow canyon that would bring the gang to the back side of the mining operation.

Walt held up his hand to stop everyone and asked if they were ready. With a murmur of agreement, the men all chambered a round in their rifles and put the hammer in a half cocked position.

Waiting patiently for Jake's diversion to start, Walt looked around at his men and thought about how rich he could become with this large of an outlaw gang and nobody to stop them. He was still considering possibilities when the distant sound of gunfire brought him back to the present. "Let's ride men!"

The riders broke their horses into a gallop. They were well into the canyon and could see the other end when gunfire suddenly erupted all around them. Three of the men were blown from their saddles before anyone had time to react.

"It's an ambush!" Walt yelled. "We can't stay here and fight, or we'll all die. Ride through as fast as you can." While the men rode hard, they fired hasty shots into the trees covering the slopes of the canyon.

Near the mouth of the canyon, Mike and Justin stood by a rock and listened to the screams of horses and dying men. Watching the survivors of the gang approaching, Mike tried to make out who the leader was. He knew the best way to break an attack was to kill the person in charge. However, the outlaws were in a panic. And with all the gunfire and the mad dash to escape, there was no way to tell who was in charge.

When the remaining outlaws were almost upon them, Mike and Justin stepped out from behind the rocks, and calmly emptied both barrels of their twelve gauge shotguns into the rapidly approaching riders. The buckshot from four barrels had a devastating effect.

One man took a direct hit to the throat and it blew his head completely off. As the head bounced to the ground, another horse reared up in panic and threw its' rider. The unfortunate outlaw hit the ground just as another horse leaped forward. Over the noise, you could hear one short anguished scream as a hoof shattered the fallen mans chest.

Dropping the shotguns, they jumped back by the rocks, grabbed their rifles and began firing at the dozen or so men who were still coming on. The outlaws had finally begun to return fire and as Mike was lining up another shot, a bullet hit him in the shoulder. Spinning with the impact and losing control of his rifle, he fell to the ground.

Seeing Mike take a hit, Justin ran forward and dragged him behind a rock as lead poured in around the two of them. Hastily firing his .45, he could hear someone yelling to keep riding and get away from the ambush. As the last of the gang rode past, Justin emptied his colt towards the departing men.

As the sound of galloping horses receded, the sudden silence in the canyon was almost deafening. Only a few minutes had gone by since the ambush had been triggered, but it seemed to have lasted for hours. Hurrying back to Mike, Justin ripped off a piece of cloth from his shirt and pressed it against Mike's wound to stop the bleeding. "How are you feeling?"

Mike groaned with pain. "How the hell do you think I'm feeling? Just take a look and see if the bullet hit a bone! I've had flesh wounds before, but this hurts like hell."

Justin kept the cloth pressed firmly down and gently

rolled Mike on his side. "It looks like the bullet went through your shoulder and shattered the collarbone on its way through. I'll need to put some sort of bandage on the exit wound also. Now hold still!" As he stopped the bleeding from that hole, he added, "You know, Mike, you're going to be one hell of a mess for the doctor to fix up."

"Thanks for the words of encouragement."

Smiling, Justin rolled Mike over on his back, and said he'd go get the rest of the men. Reloading his .45, he headed back into the canyon and shouted for the men to come on down.

*

As the gang left the canyon at a hard gallop, Walt looked around and realized Matt had not been one of the survivors. Cursing out loud, he yelled to his men. "I'm taking four men with me and get the gold moved. The rest of you continue on and join up with Jake. From here on out, kill anyone you see. Is that understood?"

With angry yelling, the rest of the men rode toward the mining office while Walt led his group through the trees and came up on the far side of the old mansion.

Stopping by the back porch, they dismounted and Walt left a man behind as a guard, while he and the other three men went into the basement and opened the secret entrance to the tunnel.

Carrying some lanterns, they hurried along the tunnel and soon came to the winches and pulleys. Sending a man over to operate the winch and roll the wall open, Walt angrily thought about the ambush. How could anyone have known the gang would be riding through that canyon? It had to be some sort of a double cross on Jeff William's part and he vowed to get even.

Inside the vault, David and the men had been having fun playing high stakes poker, when suddenly the west wall began to tremble. Looking up in astonishment, the men froze.

"Quick," David hissed. "Grab your shotguns and turn off the lanterns." Waiting in silence, the men listened to the faint sound of something moving. In the darkness they couldn't see anything, but seconds later a thin shaft of light became visible, coming from the right corner of the vault.

As the band of light became wider, the men watched in amazement as the whole wall slowly slid past them. As the gap widened they could hear voices coming from the other side. When the gap opened further, they saw three men silhouetted in the light.

When the wall stopped moving, a fourth man stepped up by the other three. This one could be heard telling the others to hurry in and start setting the gold in the tunnel. As they stepped into the vault, their lanterns cast enough light for them to finally see David and his men waiting in the far shadows.

Swearing, they grabbed for their guns. Before they were able to draw, David shouted to open fire. The hapless thieves had no chance with their bodies outlined against the light. The blast of buckshot from several shotguns fired at once, shredded through the intruders. In a fraction of a second, the men were ripped apart and slammed back into the tunnel.

While everyone's ears were still ringing from the blast, David lit his lantern. Setting it on a crate, he ran forward and began stomping out the burning kerosene from the outlaws broken lanterns. Recovering from the noise and shock, everyone else hurried over to help.

When the fire from the spilt kerosene was under control, David got his lantern and walked into the tunnel to see if anyone was still alive. The first three men were already visiting old acquaintances in hell, but the man who had been giving orders was somehow still alive...barely.

As David leaned over to see if he could do anything for the man, or get any information from him, he heard him whisper, "This wasn't how the plan was supposed to go." As Walt finished speaking, his head slumped over.

Looking around at the carnage his men had done to the outlaws, David shook his head slowly. "No, I don't imagine dying is what your plans were for today."

*

Listening to the sound of gunfire erupting from the other end of town, and shortly after from the canyon, Brad and Jason stepped up to the edge of the building and looked out. Not sure where they would be the most help, Jason suggested they stay put for the moment and see what developed. Brad didn't care for the idea of not doing anything, but knew it would be a mistake to start running around now, so he went along with Jason.

With the sound of heavy gunfire, men who had been sleeping in the bunkhouse across from the mining office came running outside with shotguns ready.

Seeing this, Brad yelled for them to find some cover and wait for his signal. Finding various places to conceal themselves, the miners nervously waited and wondered what the hell was going on.

As the sound of gunfire ended in the canyon, half a

dozen men came galloping from that direction towards the buildings where Brad and Jason were waiting. Brandishing rifles and yelling, they rapidly closed the distance. Not seeing anyone, the men continued riding toward town to meet up with Jake.

With no warning, Brad and Jason raised their rifles and took careful aim at the men. "You take the first one on the left," Brad said, "and I'll take the man on the right." When the outlaws were within range, Brad yelled, "Fire!"

Jason's bullet took his man through the chest and sent him flying backwards off his horse. Brad took out his with a clean head shot.

When the last of these outlaws slowed to return fire at Brad and Jason, the miners who had been waiting in concealment stood and opened up with a barrage of shotguns.

The remaining four men caught in the deadly crossfire didn't have a chance, and died without comprehending this second ambush.

There was still gunfire coming from town, but here the eerie silence seemed anti-climactic. Other than two horses that had to be put out of their suffering, there were no other injuries.

When the miners walked across the opening to look at the dead men, Brad told them to keep an eye out for any more outlaws. Having given them instructions, Brad yelled for Jason to follow him, and they ran off in the direction of town.

***

Jim had been waiting patiently in the alley while he watched early risers starting another work day. Shortly after six thirty, someone walked across from the hotel and entered the Land & Title office. He had never seen Jeff Williams, but he assumed this was the man. Jim noticed he didn't put up the "open" sign and the window shades stayed down.

While he debated going in and confronting William's, the sound of gunfire and yelling broke the morning silence. Quickly making sure there was a round in the chamber of his rifle, he looked down the street where he could see several men riding up it.

They appeared to be carelessly shooting at buildings and people. One person walking along the boardwalk had simply stopped to see what all the commotion was about. He never lived long enough to realize his mistake, as a stray bullet slammed into his forehead and sent bone and brains spraying out the back of his head.

Jim glanced one more time at the closed up Land & Title office. There was still no sign of activity, so he turned his attention back to the outlaws and began firing. He managed to kill one man, and wound another, before they realized someone was returning fire.

Once Jim's position had been identified, the outlaws sent a hail of gunfire towards him. Knowing the packing crates he was hiding behind wouldn't stop the bullets for long; he quickly snapped off several rounds and then ran back through the alley and in between two buildings.

Peering around a corner, he could see the men going back to shooting up the town. Sighting in on a rider who had stopped to reload, Jim shot him through the chest.

As the man fell, a second story window broke, and he could hear a rebel yell. Looking up Jim saw someone in town had decided enough was enough, and had begun laying down a field of fire.

Cheered on by the fact he was no longer alone, Jim continued to fire at the remaining outlaws. By now, there were only two outlaws still on horseback and they soon realized it would be suicide to continue. Turning their horses, they fled.

Hearing gunfire from the north of town, Jim figured the Johansen brothers were taking care of business on their end, so he decided to head back to the house and see if Marge was okay. Heading up the street, he heard people yelling questions at him, but he ignored them and continued running.

*

After Brad and Jason had left the house that morning, Marge went around and made sure weapons were where she wanted them. Then she unlocked the back door and placed a pan with silverware in front of it. She wanted advance notice of anyone entering through the kitchen, but there was no sense in making them break the door down.

Once everything was to her satisfaction, she poured a cup of coffee and splashed a small shot of brandy in it. Not knowing how the day would turn out, she thought, "What the hell," and found Brad's cigar box. After lighting one, she walked over and sat by a window where she could watch the trail up to the house.

Sitting there in the quiet room, Marge thought about what she wanted from life. She had led an adventurous one…that was for sure, but then Jim had come along. Spending years with a man like him had a certain appeal to it, and she also knew her days as a Pinkerton agent were numbered.

If they lived through the day, she would like to go see the secluded log cabin he had told her about. It sounded like a lovely place…maybe a house that could become a home for the two of them.

Reflecting on these pleasant thoughts, she was dimly aware of the grandfather's clock beginning to chime seven, when suddenly all hell seemed to break loose.

From the other end of town she could hear the sound of gunfire. These shots were soon joined by the unmistakable sounds of rifle fire and shotguns coming from the canyon that Jim had wanted an ambush set up in.

Putting out the cigar, and quickly finishing her coffee, Marge snapped open the shotgun one more time and confirmed there was a shell in each chamber. Opening the window so she could hear better, she listened and waited. Several minutes went by before the sound of gunfire began tapering off.

While she was wondering whether she should have gone along with Jim, she heard horses galloping. The sound seemed to be coming from the blind side of the house. Running through the parlor and into another room where she could get a view of that area, she heard the pan of silverware clattering across the kitchen floor.

Stopping, and stepping quietly back to the edge of the doorway, Marge waited with the shotgun leveled at her hip. Keeping a firm grip on it, she stood there patiently. A moment later, two men came out of the kitchen and stopped in the hallway.

She quickly recovered from her surprise at seeing

some of the men who had wanted to rape her at the way station and fired just one barrel. The men were standing so close to each other that the buckshot ripped through both of them. Screams of pain as the pellets tore flesh apart, turned into whimpered moans before the men fainted, or died...she didn't really care which.

Hearing someone yelling from the front door area, she replaced the spent shell and slipped back into the parlor. Staying close to the wall, she ignored the man's attempt to get his partners to answer him. Finally, he stopped shouting and she could hear soft footsteps getting closer to the parlor door.

Holding her breath, Marge watched as the barrel of a hand gun slowly slid into view from behind the door. Realizing this was her best chance; she pointed the shotgun about a foot behind the exposed revolver, and squeezed the two triggers. She hated having both of the barrels empty at the same time, but she didn't know how thick the door was, and couldn't afford to take chances.

Apparently there were enough pellets to do the job, because a hole exploded in the middle of the door, followed by the bloody scream of a man finding his midsection disappearing in a spray of flesh and blood.

Marge quickly looked around, and could see no one else, or hear anyone. She had just broken open the shotgun and extracted the spent shells when she heard a soft chuckle behind her. Whirling, she swung the shotgun like it was a baseball bat, but the man easily grabbed the barrel with his hand and jerked it away from her.

"Now that's not a very sociable way to greet an old friend," Leo said. Covering her with his .45, he leered at Marge. "Since you killed my partners, I guess I won't have to share you with them." Grinning, he pointed at the stairs and told her to start walking. "We'll find a nice comfortable place to teach you some manners."

Seething at her costly mistake, she began climbing the stairs. She still had the derringer in her pocket, but he would stop her if she suddenly grabbed for it. All she could do was bide her time and wait for him to let his guard down. Deciding to try and distract him by talking, she said, "I'm surprised to see you here. You must be part of the gang that's involved with the killings and the gold theft."

Feeling sure of himself, Leo bragged, "You're damn right I am, and when we're through with this town, we'll take what's left of the gold and be set for life. But don't worry sweet thing, if you're real good in bed maybe I'll let you live and take you along with me."

Reaching the top of the stairs, Marge paused and turned. As he stepped close to her, she could smell the rotten breath of bad teeth, tobacco, and alcohol. Fighting the gagging sensation that almost overwhelmed her; she smiled and put her right hand on his forearm. "If you're half the man I think you are, maybe we could even be partners?"

Mistaking the subtle insult for a compliment, Leo grinned. "Maybe we could, but first I'm going to get your clothes off, then have my way with you and teach you a lesson. I still owe you for making us back down at the way station."

Knowing there wasn't any way she could risk getting cornered in a bedroom, Marge put her left hand on her breasts. The sight of her hand there riveted his attention. Smiling coyly, she asked, "You'd like to hold these in your hands, wouldn't you?"

Almost shaking with anticipation, Leo nodded. "Now

just turn around and head into the nearest bedroom. I want to be done with you before the rest of the gang finishes their job and gets here."

"Oh, I think we'll have plenty of time to do what we want. Fingering her cleavage to keep his eyes focused there, Marge slammed her left knee into his groin. As her knee connected, she slapped the barrel of the gun away from her.

With a startled cry of pain, Leo squeezed the trigger but the bullet went harmlessly into the wall. Grabbing his crotch, he bellowed in agony. Swearing, he reached out with one hand and tried to grab Marge, but she wasn't waiting for him to recover.

Quickly stepping in close, she pushed him hard, and stumbling back, he hit the balcony rail. With his mind on the pain, and the momentum of the push, Leo lost his sense of balance and flipped over the railing.

Trembling with relief and anger, she walked to the edge of the balcony and looked over. Leo had hit his head on the corner of a heavy chest and his neck was twisted at an odd angle. Slowly catching her breath, she went into the bedroom and picked up her rifle.

While walking carefully downstairs, she heard someone running up onto the front porch. Making sure there was a bullet in the chamber, she stepped over the dead man and slipped behind a door.

Suddenly, she heard her name shouted and realized it was Jim calling her. With tears of relief and joy, she ran down the hall to greet him.

Cautiously coming through the front door, and pausing when he saw what was left of the man blown apart by the twin blasts of the shotgun, Jim heard Marge call back to him. Looking up as she ran around a corner, he holstered his .45 and ran forward to embrace her.

Clinging to one another, they kissed passionately. Finally they paused and she asked how things had gone in town. After telling what had happened to each other, Jim suggested they ride down to the mining office and see how things had gone there.

Making sure all the guns were loaded, Marge and Jim went to the stable and saddled up their horses. Riding down to where the rest of the men should be, she asked if he had seen Jeff Williams.

"I saw a man go into the Title Company shortly before all the shooting started...I guess it was him. After the last two outlaws fled town, I was concentrating on getting back to you and forgot all about him."

"Well, I think we had better find him before going to the mining office," Marge said. I'd hate to have that bastard skip town when he finds out we're still alive!"

Jim agreed and commented that there had been no gunshots heard for a while, so the ambushes must have been successful. They still rode cautiously however, in case Williams still had an ace up his sleeve.

Marge suggested they dismount a few buildings away and approach on foot. After tying their horses, they scanned the street for any sign of remaining outlaws, but the only people milling around were town folk surveying the damage.

Walking quietly up to the office door, Jim tried to turn the knob, but it was locked. Wondering whether he should kick the door open or not, Marge stepped up.

"Jeff hasn't met you, let me call to him." Knocking on the door, she yelled, "Jeff William's! Can you hear me?"

They could hear someone moving around inside and then a voice asked who was out there.

"It's Marge McClair! We met yesterday when Brad showed me around town. Are you all right?"

"I'm fine," Jeff shouted back. "I've stayed locked up

214

in here ever since that gang rode into town. Is it safe to come out?"

Marge looked at Jim and rolled her eyes. "What a sleazebag he is," she whispered. "He's the one who brought the outlaws here, and now he's acting like it was some horrible surprise. But let's play along with Jeff though, until we can get the drop on him, okay?" After Jim nodded his head in agreement, she yelled back that the outlaws were dead, or gone, and it was safe to open up.

When Jeff unlocked the door and began to open it, Jim slammed into the door as hard as possible. With a crash, Jeff went flying back into a desk. Jim stepped through the door and picked up the gun Jeff had dropped.

With a dazed look on his face, Jeff asked what the hell that was for.

"I'll tell you," Marge spoke up. "We know all about the Big Sky Company, and Jim saw Jacob ride out and deliver a message to the gang yesterday. Also, Justin saw Jacob leave here just before two men tried to kill Jason and me at the old mansion. If that isn't enough, we know the telegraph operator is in your pocket and so is Mr. Hartman."

Licking his lips nervously, Jeff looked back and forth at them. "Jacob runs errands for a lot of people in town. That doesn't prove anything," he said defiantly.

"Maybe it's only circumstantial evidence," Jim spoke harshly, "but I think out here on the frontier, common sense will prevail and you'll be swinging from a tree before long. However, before we get into what's going to happen, I want you to open the safe. We're going to take a look at what's in there."

"You can't make me open the safe! I own a business here, and the safe is my personal property. I know my rights and you need a warrant. Besides, you're not even the law."

"You don't want to know the kind of legal authority I have," Jim stated coldly.

"I demand that I be taken back to Helena for any possible charges," Jeff blustered.

Marge glanced over at Jim with disgust on her face. "Listen to this jackass talk about rights." She turned back to Jeff, "Right now you have an appointment to keep in hell. I would suggest you start doing anything you can think of to convince us otherwise. Now, open the safe or we'll get some dynamite from the mines and do it the hard way."

Stumbling to his feet, Jeff cursed everybody he could think of and made his way to the safe. Spinning the tumblers, he began to open the door when Jim stopped him.

Pulling Jeff back from the safe, he told Marge to keep him covered. As she pushed Jeff down into a chair, Jim pulled open the door and saw a loaded pistol lying on the middle shelf. Picking it up, he turned and asked Jeff if he really thought he could have taken both of them by surprise.

"It was worth a try," he answered in a subdued voice.

Setting the gun down, Jim looked back in the safe and noticed a blanket on the bottom shelf. Removing it, he began laughing when he saw a stack of gold bars. "I suppose these bars are also your personal property?" Getting no response from Jeff, he added, "I can't wait to hear your explanation for this."

In desperation, Jeff asked, "Isn't there some arrangement we could make? The Johansen brothers will kill me for sure when they find out about this. What if I let you take the gold, and in exchange you don't say anything? Then I could simply vanish and go back to Helena. I'd promise to keep my mouth shut."

Just then, the sound of rapid boot steps were heard coming up the boardwalk. A moment later, Brad and Jason hurried through the door. Taking in the scene in front of them, Brad said, "I see you got Williams. Has he confessed to hiring the shooter, or knowing anything about the missing gold?"

Reaching into the safe, Jim picked up a bar of gold and held it up for the brothers. "He won't confess to anything, but a minute ago he tried to bribe us with this."

Jason stepped forward and took the bar from Jim. Looking at it closely, he turned back to Jeff. "I suppose you minted this in your spare time, huh? This is our gold, you son of a bitch."

When he raised the bar as if to hit Jeff; Brad reached out and grabbed his arm. "Don't Jason. He'll pay for this later today. Besides, we don't want him unconscious when he hangs."

Taking a deep breath, Jason lowered the bar. "You're right. I want him to be painfully aware of the next few hours. Hanging's too good for you, Jeff! To think of all the innocent people who have died as a result of your scheming. However, hanging appears to be our only option, short of using some Indian techniques for really making you suffer." By now there was sheer panic on Jeff's face.

Curious about the rest of the gang, Marge interrupted. "What happened with the other ambushes?"

Forgetting about Jeff for the moment, Brad turned and smiled. "Everything worked perfectly. The only serious injury was a shoulder wound Mike suffered. Justin has him over at the doc's right now, and David is having all the dead outlaws taken out into the valley for burial. What about you two?"

After they took turns telling their stories, Jim suggested Jeff should be locked up under guard until he could be hung. "I think it would be fitting if he had to wait in the vault. He can have time to look around at all the gold and consider if his actions were worth it?"

"That sounds like a great idea," Marge said, and then added. "You do realize Brad and Jason, that all of the property purchased by Jeff was paid for with your gold, don't you?"

"That hasn't escaped our attention," Brad said sourly. Turning his attention back to Jeff, he asked how the gold was converted into currency, because all the land transactions were in cash.

Sounding defeated, Jeff said listlessly, "The leader of the gang, Walt, would take four or five bars at a time into Helena. I had a contact who would give me seventy cents on the dollar. It was a steep fee, but I figured what the hell, the gold was almost free. Then as land came up for sale, I would use the cash to make all the purchases. Does that satisfy you?" he asked with a trace of his former belligerence.

"You had a pretty smooth operation going on here," Jim commented, "but why didn't you file the quit claim deeds at the county courthouse? Marge said she found a whole stack of them in a folder."

"Because, somebody in Helena might have realized the Big Sky Company was just a front for me."

"I have an idea," Marge said thoughtfully. "Since Jeff didn't file the paperwork, and the people were paid with

218

money from you Johansen brothers, then it seems to me we could just destroy those quit claim deeds, and the Johansen Mining Company could file on them as abandoned properties. There would be a filing fee of course, but you would essentially get most of your money back in the form of land and buildings."

Jason grinned, and looked at Brad. Pretty soon they both burst out laughing, and Brad replied, "This isn't what we had in mind when we wanted to recover the missing gold, but there is a certain irony to it all."

"Excuse me for interrupting," Jim said, "But there's a small canyon that branches off the main valley, maybe two miles up the west side. There's a log cabin on it already, and I'd like to buy it."

"Buy it?" Brad said, "Hell, if you hadn't seen the gang getting ready to ride and warned us, we'd never stood a chance against a group of outlaws that big. You can file a claim on it, and consider that as payment for everything you've done. Is that okay with you, Jason?"

"It sure is, and I know which place you mean. That land belonged to Mr. Ashcroft. He lived up there for years, long before we opened up the mines again. I've been out there and it's a beautiful house. He must have been an exceptional craftsman, judging from the quality of the construction. Unfortunately, he was found murdered two years ago."

Jeff started laughing hysterically, "He's the crazy old coot who told me about the secret entrance. After the mines were opened up and I moved out here, I traveled around visiting all the properties. When I talked to him about the valley and the mines, he began reminiscing.

After a few shots of whiskey, he loosened up and began talking about a tunnel from the old owner's house to the basement of the mining office. He had been in charge of the construction and knew all the details. That information gave me the idea of eventually taking over the valley and using your money to pay for it."

Brad walked over and backhanded Jeff across the face. "You had a harmless old man killed, just to make sure he didn't tell anyone else about the tunnel? Get him out of here, Jason. He makes me sick!"

After tying Jeff's hands behind his back, so he could not try anything, Jason led him out the door and headed for the mining office.

"Well," Marge said, "I think the last thing we need to do is wire Wilson that everything is under control here."

"What are you going to do about the telegraph operator?" Jim asked. "He'll just warn Mr. Hartman."

"At this point, there's nothing Hartman could do to help Jeff. Besides, I'll send the message myself."

"Let's get it done," Brad said. "Then I'll have some men put together a makeshift gallows and we can hang Jeff this afternoon."

Walking towards the telegraph office, they were asked by several people what was going on. Brad told them to come up to the north end of town at two o'clock and he would explain everything.

As they stepped into the telegraph office, the operator stood up and asked if he could help them. Jim pulled out his gun and told him he was no longer working there and suggested he leave town...permanently.

"You can't come in here and make me leave," he said indignantly. "I work for the telegraph company."

"Not anymore," Marge replied. "When we were in the other day, I asked you to send messages to Wilson, and Callie. You addressed both of them to Mr. Hartman,

220

so we know you were in with Jeff Williams." Smiling, she added, "You didn't count on someone showing up and knowing Morse code, did you?"

Crestfallen, the man asked if he could at least send one more message.

"I don't think so," Marge said. "I'll send it, and I'd advise you to leave town before we decide to hang you too!"

Nervously looking at the hard look Brad was giving him; the operator grabbed his coat and fled the office.

Marge then went to the telegraph keys and wired the Governor. In the message, she informed him about their success, and explained about Mr. Hartman's connection. Then she sent another wire to Callie. In this one, she explained she planned on staying out here permanently with Jim and would be quitting the Pinkerton's.

When she had finished, Brad found a key and locked the door to the telegraph office. While Brad walked back to the mining office, they got their horses and rode over to the Johansen house.

As they were riding, Jim asked her about the second message she had sent.

Not sure how to start, she finally told him that living out here with him was something she really wanted to do. "After all, I said you would have to make an honest woman out of me someday, remember?"

Laughing, he reached out his hand for hers. "I'd be honored to have you share my last name...legally. Although, I must say this is the strangest wedding proposal I've ever heard of. Isn't the man supposed to ask the woman?"

"Times are changing, Jim. Women are going to start demanding an equal say in all matters. Not just cook, clean, and have babies for their men. Why, someday there might even be a woman Governor."

"I can't see that ever happening," he replied. "But let's not get into social or political discussions, when we should be thinking about plans for moving to our new home."

With a mischievous smile from Marge, they stopped talking and rode the rest of the way in happy silence.

Before long, word spread through town about the gang getting wiped out, and Jeff William's role in the whole operation. If he hadn't been under lock and key, the towns' people would probably have strung him up on the spot. However, the Johansen brothers promise that Jeff would hang at two o'clock kept a lynch mob under control.

When the hanging was about a half hour away; Brad, along with Justin, and David, went to get Jeff from the vault. As they began escorting him down the street towards the gallows, the foreman for the Rocking Chair P ranch rode up with several men.

Seeing Jeff tied up, and being prodded along with the barrel of a rifle, the foreman brought his horse to a halt and asked what the hell was going on.

Brad rested his hand on his .45 and told the foreman what had transpired and why Jeff was about to be hung.

"You can't just hang a man without a trial," the foreman snapped. "Besides, Jeff's a silent owner in the ranch and Mr. Conroy won't let this happen."

Brad looked around with a smile on his face. "Well, I don't see your boss around, and if he was, I could probably get some volunteers to hang him too."

"What the hell are you talking about?" the foreman almost screamed.

"I mean that Mr. Conroy knew all about what was happening in the valley. So by rights, he's just as guilty. Now, before I get really pissed off, and decide you and your men knew about everything also, I want you to get the hell out of town and tell Mr. Conroy some men and I will be coming by for a visit. Tell him I'll be making an offer on his ranch and he'd better not even think of turning it down!"

Looking around at his men, who were starting to get nervous, the foreman tried to sound tough. "You try to take that ranch and there'll be a lot of blood on your hands. We have a small army available to defend it!"

Justin cleared his throat, "I don't think you were paying attention to what Brad said. And that "small army" has already been buried out in the valley, with the only survivors probably half way to Helena by now."

As the implication sunk in, the other ranch hands began looking around and realized there were numerous miners standing close by, and every one of them was armed with shotguns.

One of the riders got his boss's attention and pointed them out. When the foreman finally noticed the armed men, his face paled and he lost any fight that might have been left in him. "Let's ride back to the ranch, men," as he gave Brad a hateful look. "We'll see what the boss wants us to do."

"You do that," Brad shouted after him. "Just be sure and tell him to sell out, or be carried out...the choice is his."

After the riders left, they continued to march Jeff toward the gallows. Taking a look at his pocket watch, Brad saw it was almost time for the scheduled hanging. "It won't be long now. Before we hang you, though, I'll give you a chance to say any last words."

"I still can't believe you're going to hang me without a real trial," Jeff cried out. "It's not fair! Why can't I have the same chance as Mr. Conroy and move out of the area?"

"Because you hired a shooter and had close to two

dozen innocent people killed," Brad replied. "And if that's all you want to rant and rave about, then I won't waste time giving you a chance to say any last words. Now shut up!"

Dejected and helpless, Jeff lowered his head and continued shuffling toward the gallows. Hearing the angry shouts of a mob, he looked up and realized they were almost there.

Armed miners were keeping the crowd about thirty feet from where a rope twisted gently in the breeze, and Jim and Marge were standing by some makeshift steps.

Stepping up on the platform, Brad waved and yelled to the crowd to shut up. After the noise and shouting died down, he explained what had happened in the early morning hours, and what part Jeff had played in all of the killings and in the theft of the gold.

With his voice getting drowned out by the renewed shouting from the angry people, Brad looked down at David and nodded for him to bring Jeff up the steps.

As David brought him forward, Jim scanned the area and looked for anyone who might be stupid enough to try and save Jeff from hanging. Past the crowd, coming from the direction of town, he could see four horsemen trotting up the street.

Raising his field glasses, Jim could see badges on the front of their dusters. Yelling over to Brad, he pointed in the direction of the riders.

Wondering why Jim was concerned about them, Brad told David to keep Jeff there and walked back down the steps. "What's going on?" he asked.

"I don't know," Jim replied, "But those men coming up the street are wearing U.S. Marshall's badges. We'd better see what they want."

225

By now, the crowd had noticed the men riding up and moved aside so they could get through. When the lawmen approached the makeshift gallows, they stopped and dismounted. One stepped forward and spoke up. "I'm Marshall Jones. We received orders to get to Deer Creek as fast as we could. What's going on here?"

Jim walked up to the Marshall and briefly explained the situation, and why Jeff was about to be hung. As Jones nodded in understanding, Jeff yelled that he had a last request. Turning to him, Jim asked what it was.

"I want to speak with the Marshall."

Looking at Brad, who simply shrugged his shoulders, Jim motioned to have Jeff brought over to where they were standing.

When Jeff was a few feet from the men, he frantically began pleading. "Listen Marshall, they're accusing me of a serious crime and planning on hanging me. But I've never been given the chance to prove my innocence at a trial. You've got to stop them!"

Jones scratched his head and thought for a moment. "I don't see what I can do. The evidence sounds pretty damning from what I've been told."

"That's just it! You're only hearing their version of what happened. I demand you take me back to Helena and turn me over for a fair trial. Besides, I'm a lawyer, and as an officer of the court I deserve special consideration. You must know, Marshall Jones; the Territorial Circuit Judge is Mr. Renslow and he would expect nothing less from a U.S. Marshall than my safe return. The whole point of law and order is to give a person their day in court!"

Shaking his head, Jones replied, "Why is it you criminals break, or twist, every law you can, and then when you're caught, immediately start talking about your legal rights?"

Interrupting, Jim reached into his pocket and pulled out the letter from Wilson, the one which made him a special deputy for the governor. Handing it over to the Marshall, he said, "I think this gives me the right to sanction this hanging."

Pausing to read the letter, the Marshall looked at Jim and then the angry crowd. "Well, Mr. McClair, this does give you sweeping authority. However, if you would give me a little time to talk with my men, I'd appreciate it."

As the Marshall and his deputies stepped off to the side and began a whispered discussion, Marge asked Jim what he thought would happen. "They can't really interfere with what we're doing, can they?"

"I don't know, Marge. These are Federal Marshall's and I really don't know the law."

Several minutes went by before Marshall Jones left his deputies and walked back to Jim. "I've talked the situation over with my men and as much as I hate doing this, we've reached the conclusion that legally we need to take this man back for trial."

As word of this spread through the crowd, the mutterings began turning into angry shouts for immediate justice. Looking around at the livid people and then at the smirk on Jeff's face, Jim turned back to the Marshall. "You can't be serious?"

Resigning himself to what looked like an ugly confrontation coming up, Jones sighed. "Try and understand our position, Mr. McClair. This is still a territory, and Federal law supercedes local law. We have to take him back. I truly am sorry about this! I wish we had arrived a

227

half hour later and then we wouldn't be in this position. But the fact is, we did arrive before the hanging, and now we have to resolve this dilemma according to the law...not our personal feelings."

Grabbing Jim's arm, Marge asked, "Is Jeff going to get away with this? Isn't there anything you can do? You know that bastard is going to get some slick attorney. By the time his lawyer gets done, Jeff will probably walk away a free man. You know how difficult it will be to prove his guilt to a jury? Hell, he'll probably convince them we planted the gold bars in his safe just to frame him."

Quietly, Jim replied, "I know how frustrating it is and I feel the same way you do. Believe me, I get so tired of criminals, or in this case lawyers, who use loop-holes in the letter of the law to subvert the spirit of the law that it makes me want to scream."

Clearing his throat, Marshall Jones interrupted, "I know how you feel, Ma'am. However, we have to do this, and while I don't know what will happen in court, I can promise you Jeff will stay locked up until the trial. Also, considering Mr. McClair's authority, we won't even have to take written affidavits from anyone. Those can wait until the prosecutor contacts people."

Turning to the crowd, the Marshall explained there would be no hanging, and whoever interfered with the duties of a Federal Marshall would also be arrested and taken back for trial.

Motioning for his deputies to take Jeff into custody, he turned to Jim and told him again how sorry he was they arrived before the hanging.

"I'm sorry you did too. We can't stop you, Marshall, so go ahead and take the prisoner."

228

As Jeff was led toward a horse, he turned back and taunted the crowd. "I'll be in jail for a few days…maybe several weeks, but this will eventually get thrown out of court, because you're right about loopholes. I know a lawyer who's so good at manipulating the letter of the law, he could convince a jury there's only six days in a week." Continuing to laugh, Jeff turned to a deputy and asked for help getting on the horse.

When the Marshall's had mounted and started riding back through town with their prisoner, Jim turned and told Marge to stay with the Johansen brothers. "I've still got something I need to take care of."

Giving him a quizzical look, she nodded as he left to get Whisper.

Riding back to the house, Jim thought about how Jeff was probably right. He would more than likely be a free man. Jeff might serve a little time in jail, but that would probably be it. The laws were becoming too complex to take into account the question of whether or not someone had actually committed the crime they were arrested for.

Shaking his head in disgust, he dismounted Whisper, and walked into the house. On the floors and walls could be seen the blood stains of the men who had tried to kill Marge. Clearing his head of any further distractions, Jim quickly went upstairs and opened the rifle case. Picking up the 45-90, he grabbed several rounds and placed them in his pocket.

Stepping quickly down the stairs, he mounted Whisper and rode back through the canyon where the bloody ambush had taken place earlier. Once he left the canyon, he circled back through a forested slope and maintained a parallel course with the road leading back to Helena.

229

Where there were occasional breaks in the tree line, he could see the road, and before long saw that he had caught up to, and passed the Marshall's group. Soon he was far enough in front so he could loop down on the road and send his horse into a gallop.

When Jim was about ten miles from the mining town, he began searching for a good site to look down on the road. He needed a vantage point where he could have a shot of at least a quarter of a mile and preferably a little further. The place also needed to have a concealed route where he would be able to exit the area without being seen by anyone.

Finally, he found the place he was looking for. There was a rocky outcropping about a hundred feet above the road and behind it the forest covered the slope in both directions. This will be perfect, he thought, as he carefully rode Whisper up into the rocks.

Dismounting, Jim led Whisper back into the trees and tied a slip knot for quick release. Using his field glasses, he surveyed the hills in both directions to decide which way would be the best for rapid and concealed travel. After making up his mind which escape route to use, he walked back to the rocky outcropping and placed a round in the chamber.

Carefully leaning the rifle against a rock, Jim studied the bend in the road with his glasses. With no sign of any movement or dust in the distance, he set the glasses down and rolled a smoke. Inhaling, he looked around the valley and was again amazed at how beautiful it was. Smoking his cigarette, and thinking about Marge, allowed him to relax and ponder his next move.

Jim knew the Marshall's were only doing their duty as they saw fit, and he didn't have a problem with that.

However, there was no way in hell Jeff was going to have a chance to get away with multiple murders. He just had to be careful not to hit the Marshall, or any of his deputies. Once he had confirmed Jeff was dead, he would have to slip back into the trees and get back to town as quickly as possible. The last thing Jim needed was to get into a confrontation with Federal authorities.

Grinding the butt of his smoke into the ground, Jim picked up his glasses and studied the road. Before too long, he could make out the lazy drift of dust coming from beyond the low foothills. Minutes later, he watched as the Marshall and his deputies rounded a bend and came into sight.

At least the Marshall was good on his word. Jeff was still bound and there were two deputies about fifteen feet in front of him. The Marshall and the other deputy were trailing the prisoner at about the same distance.

Setting down the glasses, Jim picked up his rifle and rested his arm on a rock for steady support. Tracking Jeff with the scope, he noticed that he appeared to be talking and laughing. Swinging the scope to the Marshall's face, he could see Jeff was being ignored.

Satisfied, Jim followed Jeff with the rifle scope and patiently waited for the men to ride farther along the road. He couldn't afford a fluke miss and have cover nearby where the Marshall's could protect their prisoner. After another hundred yards or so, he decided they were too far from reaching safety in case he needed to take a second shot.

After taking one more look at the smug expression on Jeff's face, he lowered the crosshairs to a spot just below his throat. Since the riders were in no hurry, he didn't have to worry about leading the shot.

Jim gently squeezed the first trigger to take up the slack in the firing mechanism. Then he slowly exhaled and pulled the second trigger. The rifle bucked in his hands, as the sharp crack of a bullet traveling faster than sound echoed through the area.

Rapidly placing another round in the rifle, he sighted back in on the group. The Marshall's had quickly dismounted, and were taking cover behind their horses while looking all around for a target.

In the center of the road was the horse Jeff had been riding. It was agitated and rearing in fear, and lying in the road was Jeff. The bullet had taken him through the chest, and even from this distance, Jim knew he had died instantly.

Quickly dropping out of sight behind the rocks, Jim picked up his field glasses and sprinted for Whisper. Once there, he mounted and rode farther into the trees before veering off on an angle to make his retreat.

Jim knew the Marshall's would wait awhile before scouting the area and he was counting on this additional time to get away. Once he was a couple miles from the scene, he slowed his horse for a breather. When Whisper was breathing normally again, he took off on a slow trot and continued back to the Johansen house.

Working his way up to the backside of the house so no would see him; he hitched Whisper to a railing and grabbed his rifle.

Entering through the back kitchen door, he could hear voices coming from the parlor. Not wanting to put anyone in the position of lying for him, he located a small side room and put the rifle in there.

Walking quietly into the parlor, he found the Johansen brothers and Marge relaxing with drinks around the fireplace.

She was the first person to see him. Setting her glass down, she rushed over and gave him a big hug. "Where did you go, Jim? We looked all over for you."

Stepping back, and accepting a glass of whiskey from Brad, he smiled, and simply told them he had had some unfinished business to take care of. It felt good having her by his side and knowing anything else that came up in the valley would be taken care of by the mining company.

Leaning back in a soft chair, Jim listened to the talk around him and occasionally answered questions, but for the most part this was a time to unwind.

Suddenly, the sound of horses galloping up the drive could be heard. Mike, with his arm and shoulder heavily bandaged, stepped over to the window. "It looks like some Marshall's."

Jason and Brad hurried over to take a look. "It's the same ones who were here earlier," Jason said. "I wonder where Jeff is."

"We'll find out," Brad replied. "But if he escaped, there's going to be hell to pay, and I don't care if they are U.S. Marshall's."

Watching Marshall Jones get off his horse and head for the porch, Brad went to meet him at the door. When the Marshall was brought into the parlor, everyone could see how angry he was.

"Where's the prisoner?" Marge demanded.

"Don't worry about him, Ma'am," Jones snapped. "Some son of a bitch shot him. He's long dead, and I want to know if anyone here knows anything about it. He was our prisoner and under the protection of U.S. Marshall's."

233

While the brothers and Marge exchanged meaningful glances, Jim spoke up. "The Territorial Governor sent me to track down a sniper who has been killing people lately. I guess he's still out there."

The Marshall was just getting ready to respond when Brad interrupted. "The Federal authorities considered the other killings to be a local problem and wouldn't help, so I suggest you leave and we'll continue to look for the shooter like we have been all summer."

As the Marshall angrily twisted his hat, he could see there would be no sympathy, or offer of help from these people. Finally, in a frustrated voice, he said. "We're going, but after I file my report, there may be a whole lot of Marshall's around here looking for the person responsible." With that, Marshall Jones turned and stomped out of the room. There was silence while everyone listened to the sound of their horses leaving.

After a few moments, Brad started laughing and winked at Jim. "Well, it's a good thing you're planning on settling down here, Jim. It'll give you plenty of time to keep looking for that mysterious shooter."

* * *

Marge and Jim wandered leisurely up the valley the next day and found the box canyon he had described to her. Entering the narrow draw, she became excited and asked if this was the only way in.

"There might be some trails a person could ride on, but as far as I know, this is the only wagon accessible approach. Why?"

"It's beautiful, and there's something so private about a home this secluded. My uncle's place back east was surrounded by farms and the only thing separating them was fences. I never really felt at ease looking across at neighbors like that. Here there are rock walls and wooded slopes instead of fences, and nobody else to look at. I love it!"

Pleased that she was happy about the isolated location, he didn't say anything else while they rode across the field. Eventually, they came to the creek and stopped to let their horse's water.

"I hope there are fish in here," he said. "I passed two boys back in Helena who were fishing and it brought back some good memories."

"I never got to go fishing when I was little," Marge said wistfully. "It wasn't considered the proper thing for young ladies to do."

"Well, I'd say you're old enough now to do whatever you want. How about after we get settled in, I find some long branches we could use as poles and we wander the creek? It will be a good way to look over the property at the same time."

"That sounds fun. Now, let's get to the cabin and check it out." Slapping her horse on the rump, it leaped forward and galloped ahead of him.

Laughing, he spurred his horse and tried to catch up to her before she could reach the house, but Marge had already dismounted before he caught up to her. Jumping off his horse, he picked her up in his arms and swirled her around. "That wasn't very fair. You got the jump on me."

Teasingly, she told him to put her down. "I didn't think the big Jim McClair could be surprised like that? Stepping back from him, she took a closer look at the house. "I thought this was a small log cabin from the way you described it, but this is huge. It must be sixty feet long!"

"I guess my description didn't do it justice. Isn't that a beautiful porch? It extends along the entire length of the house, and will be a peaceful place to sit and look out over the fields."

"Let's go inside," Marge said. Walking up to the door, she paused and read the notice from the Big Sky Company. "Well, we can rip this down." Reaching for the door latch, she was surprised it opened up. "How come there's no lock on the door?"

"These homes are spread so far apart that if someone wanted to get in, they would just break a window or kick the door in, and no one would notice...so why bother with a lock."

Nodding her head, she stepped through the entrance and stood speechless. There was a massive fireplace at each end of the house and in the center was a finely crafted wood table that would easily seat a dozen people.

Beyond the table was a kitchen that looked out on the wooded slope to the rear of the canyon. She could only imagine what this looked like during the winter, with a blanket of snow covering everything. "Oh Jim, this is incredible!"

Smiling, he took her hand and led her down to one of the fireplaces. Walking beneath the vaulted beams, he pointed out a door to a room. "Mr. Ashcroft was really into symmetry. Did you notice there is an identical door down by the other fireplace and the kitchen is centered in the cabin?"

"I noticed that. Look Jim, there above the fireplace is a deer antler rifle rack."

Pausing, he studied it for a moment. "I'll be right back." While she continued to admire the spacious room, he left and returned a moment later carrying his rifle case. Setting it on a table, he opened it up and carefully lifted the 45-90 out.

"Sometime you need to tell me about that rifle and some of your other adventures," Marge commented.

"I will one day, but for now I'd like to put the rifle somewhere and stop carrying it with me every place I go."

Placing it on the antler rack, he stepped back. "Hopefully, the next time I take it down will be to hunt elk. Wouldn't it be nice if we could just settle down and enjoy each other and life in the valley...maybe take an occasional trip to a city?"

Taking his hand in hers, she looked at him with a twinkle in her eyes. "We have plenty of time to discuss the future. For now, why don't we see if one of those doors leads to a bedroom...?"

Coming soon
The exciting adventures continue with Jim McClair in

Puritan Falls

...We don't serve hard liquor in Puritan Falls and only men are allowed in here," he responded in a louder than necessary voice. Then in a soft whisper, he asked if they had just come in on the train.

Jim and Marge glanced at each other with puzzled expressions on their faces and she nodded slightly.

The bartender continued in a low voice, "I suggest you leave and get back to the train." Then he switched back to a normal level, "I told you women aren't allowed in here, so she's going to have to leave!"

Jim was getting tired of this whole nonsense and was about to tell the bartender what he thought when the distant sound of a trains' whistle could be heard. Quickly reaching for his pocket watch, he checked the time and saw it still showed eleven thirty. "Damn," he snapped, "the stupid watch stopped working!" Turning to the bartender, Jim asked brusquely what time it was.

Seeing the cold look in the strangers' eyes, he hastily answered, "It's one o'clock."

"Son of a bitch," Marge said in disgust, "the train is supposed to leave at one!"

Jim grabbed her arm and they ran from the saloon towards the train station. People were now openly staring at them, but neither one noticed as they hurried down the street. When they were still three blocks from the station, Jim knew it was too late because he could here the sound of the train beginning to pick up speed. Realizing they could never get there in time, he pulled Marge to a stop and caught his breath.

"I'm sorry, sweetheart. Who would have thought the watch would quit working in the middle of this god forsaken place?"

After Marge's breathing had returned to normal, she hugged him, "It's okay; I know you didn't do it on purpose."

Jim couldn't help laughing, "That's for damn sure! A town that serves nothing but beer...and only to men is not the place I'm going to try and surprise you with a good time."

Since it was obvious they would have to spend the next night or two in Puritan Falls until the next northbound train came along, Jim became more philosophical about the situation and told her they might as well see if there was any place to get a room for the night...

...Jim and Marge both signed in the book and then the man looked at the signatures and stated in a shocked voice, "You have different last names, aren't the two of you married?"

"What the hell difference does that make?" Jim snapped as he laid a half-eagle on the counter.

The man's eyes lit up for a moment at the sight of gold, but then they lost their luster, and he said in a resigned voice, "You're not supposed to swear either."

Jim had lost all patience by now, "What the hell is wrong with this place?"

The man got a sad look in his eyes and tried to explain, "Puritan Falls has very strict rules regarding personal behavior. Morality is the foundation upon which all great civilizations are built," he mindlessly intoned, as if it was something he had heard so often that it was

239

memorized. "Our society has…"

"Shut up," Jim ordered. "No one is going to interfere with my personal choices or lifestyle. Now give me the key to the room!"

The man glanced up and cringed at the cold fury in Jim's eyes. "Here's the key, Mr. McClair." He started to suggest they reconsider sharing the same room, when he got a faraway look in his eyes and said softly, "I don't think it would matter anyway, though."

"What do you mean by that?" Marge asked.

"Nothing," he answered, "I hope everything turns out well for you here in Puritan Falls," and then he turned and disappeared into the back room.

Jim shook his head and looked at Marge, "Well, I guess I should have known something like this would happen."

"Why do you say that?" she asked as they headed for the stairs.

"As I was falling asleep last night on the train, my last thoughts were how everything was going so perfect on the trip back to Helena."

She gave his arm a squeeze, "Oh Jim, don't be such a pessimist."

His somber mood had disappeared and he laughed. "The glass is always half-full in my mind, dear, so I am an optimist. The only difference for me is that I'm expecting someone to try and knock it over."

Marge busted out laughing, "Oh, I get it! You're a paranoid optimist."

The lighthearted banter had eased the tension they had been under since their arrival in Puritan Falls and they soon forgot about the weird little town they were in. Reaching their room, Jim unlocked the door…